Mary Cecil Hay

Under the Will and Other Tales

Vol. 1

Mary Cecil Hay

Under the Will and Other Tales
Vol. 1

ISBN/EAN: 9783337342678

Printed in Europe, USA, Canada, Australia, Japan

Cover: Foto ©Andreas Hilbeck / pixelio.de

More available books at **www.hansebooks.com**

UNDER THE WILL

AND

OTHER TALES.

BY

MARY CECIL HAY,

AUTHOR OF

"OLD MYDDELTON'S MONEY,"
"NORA'S LOVE TEST,"
&c. &c.

IN THREE VOLUMES.
VOL. I.

LONDON:
HURST AND BLACKETT, PUBLISHERS,
13, GREAT MARLBOROUGH STREET.
1878.

LONDON:
PRINTED BY DUNCAN MACDONALD,
BLENHEIM HOUSE.

UNDER THE WILL.

PART I.

FROM HOPE WYNNE'S DIARY.

"The steersman Time sits hidden astern,
  With dark hand plying the rudder of doom."
                                    SWINBURNE.

Thursday, June 28th, 1868.

"IT might be the Field of the Cloth of Gold," said Charlie.

I was perched on the gate above that sloping field of buttercups, and Charlie was astride upon one post, while Alan leaned against the gate upon my other side. It was just as we had spent many an hour, talking or thinking, in the old days when Charlie and Alan were papa's

B 2

pupils, and I the only child of the house, loved them both so dearly as big brothers. It all seemed just the same, though I am eighteen now, and they are twenty-three, and live away in a different world from mine, only coming home (they still call the vicarage *home*) now and then for a little rest or holiday. I forget these differences as we idle together in the old spots just as we used to do, and I forget even the shadows on their lives—I mean Charlie's want of success in his profession, and the terrible disappointment Alan suffered when the aunt, who had promised his dying father years ago that she would amply provide for him, died and left him only £300. What a fortune for a gentleman to face the world with—having no knowledge of a profession, and no preparation for any special career!

But, as I say, I forget all this, in my great enjoyment of this Summer holiday, when we are all day long together, just as we used to be.

" What splendid races we used to have, down this field and through the orchard into the vicarage garden," I said.

" Always jumping at last over that one long garden bed which was your special property, Hope," added Alan, " in Spring a creeping flame of gilly-flower, and in the Autumn holidays a wilderness of asters."

" And which we two always weeded and planted for you, like the slaves we were," put in Charlie, bending forward that his quizzical blue eyes might take in my reception of this original remark.

" You may well say *were*," I answered, with excessive gravity. " Who would now think that you had either of you been good-natured *once*?"

" We did all our weeding and planting in those old days," Charlie went on. " Now, of course, we expect only to reap."

Then we were silent again, as we often are, we three, and the shadows flitted softly from our feet along the golden floor of buttercups. Ah! what a noon it was! I think there are days when one's whole past life seems stirred within one, and there come to the surface unlooked-for visions and pictures and gleams from the depths below. Are they of Memory, or of Hope? or is it possible that those two words mean one thing only, and *are* one at last, when our lives are rounded and complete. This was one of those glad, *living* days; just as yesterday, still and shrouded as it was beneath its clouds, was a day of deepest thought. Nature herself lay at rest, only waiting—waiting.

"If I ever travel far away," said Charlie, and his words seemed to fit into the silence, instead of breaking it, "what a picture I shall always carry in my mind of this quiet home of ours."

He was looking down upon the ivied and gabled walls of the old vicarage, but I was looking at him, and I noticed that just then that shadow fell across his face which we have never liked to see, and which terribly reminds me—though I could never speak of this—how very young his parents died.

But I only said quite comfortably, "It looks as picturesque as if the rain didn't pour into every room on a wet day."

"That used to be great fun," laughed Charlie. "How Alan and I used to fly from room to room with pails and cloths. And I well remember carrying your father's bath to the drawing-room to catch the shower from the top of the bow window, and your insisting on our carrying *you* in the bath, Hope."

"Yes, I remember."

"Do you like that new game we sent you, Hope?" asked Alan, presently. "Croquet they call it."

"I think it would be tremendously nice and exciting, if played on a rather level lawn—at any rate, on ground *inclining* towards level. On our hill-side lawn I find it—confusing, Alan."

"Oh! we will fix it presently," he answered, laughing, "and give you a fair

chance of judging. Who is that in the
porch?"

It was papa, halting to see that his net
was right before he started off on his
almost daily hunt for butterflies; and behind him mamma came out, in her garden
bonnet and gloves, and with a watering-
can in her hand. They stopped a few
minutes talking together in the shade of
the quaint old porch, where the roses
cling so lightly to the sturdy ivy, and
shower their dainty perfumed kisses among
its gnarled old roots, while above all the
wooden cross stands clearly outlined
against the Summer sky. Then papa went
on, in his big felt hat, and with his net on
his shoulder; and mamma was speedily lost
to sight in her tiny greenhouse.

"I could alter Burns' lines for our mother, Hope," Charlie said, with the merry
twinkle in his eyes. "I am sure that
for *her* 'happiness has its seat and centre
in the'—garden." Charlie always speaks of
my father and mother as his, and no won-

der, when he has been an orphan from
babyhood.

"I must go and help her," I said, with
a new impulse.

"I would work hard to dissuade her,"
Charlie said, apostrophising the sky in
a most provoking way, just because I
did not jump up at once, "only I know
she has not the faintest intention of
going. She looks the very personification
of idleness this moment."

"My day's work is over now, until the
afternoon, when I must go into the village."

"I shall come," put in Charlie in haste;
and just then Alan looked up and met my
eyes, and paused in the words he had
more quietly begun to say.

"*You* are idle, Alan," I said, speaking
almost nervously, though I cannot even
now imagine why, "or you would offer to
come too."

"He is allowed to be idle," interposed
Charlie, interrupting Alan's answer.

"Poets always are—witness Petrarch."

"If Petrarch had been really idle, he would have written *no* poetry, would he, Alan ?" I asked, with a glance at Charlie, because I was confident *he* had never written any. And then I enquired anxiously of Alan if his poetry were better than it used to be.

"Pathos is his strong point," put in Charlie, in his debonair way, so merry, yet always so gentle. "Listen reverentially, Hope, and I will give you a specimen of his style. *You* may possibly think it ambiguous, but, bless you, that's its beauty. He always holds manfully to the poetic laws, which are three : firstly, always begin each verse with an *O,* long drawn out ; secondly, always end it with a note of exclamation ; and thirdly, never let cheerfulness creep in, under penalty of degenerating into prose."

"Go on," said Alan, laughing heartily—for we never laugh at each other any more readily than we laugh at ourselves, and he was as much amused as I was at the notion of hearing Charlie improvise.

"As thus," observed Charlie, clearing his throat, and lifting his eyes enthusiastically to the little white clouds, that wouldn't wait to be looked at; while he made a lengthened pause on the first word of every verse—

> "O— the sighing and the crying!
> O— the weeping *and* the tears!
> O— the cheerfulness of dying
> Long before we're strick'n in years!
>
> "O— the wither'd, wither'd flowers!
> O— the weeping, weeping skies!
> O— those damp, unhealthy bowers,
> Where we're eaten up by flies!
>
> "O— the cowslip-cover'd meadow!
> ˙ O— the wet and wand'ring wave!
> O— the sunshine and the shedow!
> O— the jovial, jovial grave!"

"Go on," laughed Alan, in his pause. "You haven't hit the spirit of the poet quite deep enough yet."

> "O— cupation? I'll not know it!
> O— my bills I will not pay!
> O— I'm such a heaven-born poet,
> That I sit and weep all day!

There, little lady, beat that if you can.
I shall publish a volume some day, and
earn a fortune by it."

"You are very fond of money, Alan," I
remarked, as solemnly as if I did not know
that if he had been even a little less in-
different about it, he would now have had
a fortune.

" 'Blessings brighten as they take their
flight,'" he quoted, laughing.

"I think," observed Charlie, in deep
thought, "that we must fall back upon the
cultivation of pigs at the Cape, Alan. I
see no plan that opens such fine prospects."

"When do you think to go?" I questioned, just as placidly as if my heart were
not beating, and my head suddenly aching,
as it always does, even at the faintest
suggestion of losing my dear companions.

"We always *think* to go," said Charlie,
with a laugh in his beautiful blue eyes.
" That's why we always stay at home."

" Thinking is such a mistake," said Alan.
" It's better not to think at all than to do
nothing beyond. And it is getting a serious
matter, Charlie. We must make some
bold stroke to bring us money."

" I hate money."

Of course that blunt and senseless remark was mine, but of course it only meant
that I hated anything which might separate
us.

"You would not hate it, Hope, dear,"
Alan said, " if you lived more in the world,
and could see its power."

" If so, I'm glad I don't live more in the
world."

Two restless brown bees dive in and
out of the long trumpets of the honey-
suckle, humming busily, to show they
really are at work, and to put out of
countenance the small white butterfly that
(watching them) skims among the leaves
so uselessly herself. But I notice that she
will not be put out, but seems to laugh,
and spreads her wings in the sunshine, as

if she understood best the task of her little life—as perhaps she does.

"So am I glad you do not live in the world," said Charlie, with a strange note of earnestness in his voice; and again that shadow of despondency, which I know so well, crosses his face.

"Yet you want to live in even a wider and a more distant one, you and Alan?"—For it was less horrible to think of both going than of Charlie going alone.

"It is not what we *want*, Hope," Alan answered, in his earnest way. "It is what will soon be a matter of necessity with us —I fear."

"Yet it was only yesterday," I fretted, "that you both said, while we were fishing, you never wanted more than what Hazlitt said contented him—food, warmth, sleep, and a book."

"But those are all costly luxuries, dear Hope," said Alan—he always seems to take a thing more seriously than Charlie does—"and the obtaining of them necessitates a good deal of hard work first."

"Cannot you earn money at home as easily as abroad?" I urged, trying to make my eyes not ask the question more anxiously of Charlie than of Alan.

"We are trying. Not long ago I answered one advertisement that offered a competency gratis, but I did not care for the career suggested. It was to sell a patent aluminium pencil-case on commission."

"If I ever had a fortune," I said, without vouchsafing a smile; and so strenuously looking away from Charlie that I fixed my eyes steadily on the tall white tower far down the valley, while that put into my head what to say, for I had not known when I began my sentence, "I should restore the old church."

I am accustomed to make speeches irrelevantly, and no one who is used to me ever wonders over it.

"I will give you your organ, Hope,"
said Alan, "as soon as ever my ship comes
home."

"What is the name of your ship?" I
asked, just still that I might not look at
Charlie. "I can watch for the arrival
when I know her name."

"*Hope*," he said, rather quietly and
gravely.

"That ship," said Charlie, with strange
haste, and springing to the ground as he
spoke, "is always homeward bound for
all of us—surely. But the vessel *our*
fortunes are to come in, Alan, is not
yet launched, I fear."

"I don't believe the trees are grown for
her timber yet, old fellow."

I was looking at them both as they
spoke, and wondering—wondering——
Then I remembered (and to me it was
just as if a ray of light had fallen suddenly amongst us) that papa had often
said "the lads" were so spirited and
so healthy, so fresh and unspoiled by

the world, that they would never be old.

"At my age," I remember his once saying, "they will be young men still."

We all started together this afternoon—just as it is so natural for us to do; but when we reached the gate between the shrubbery path and the lane, Alan stayed on the inner side, and only nodded a good-bye to me when I looked back surprised. But somehow this seemed so unusual that I waited, looking I'm sure the question I did not ask.

"I am going down to the ferry," he said. "Bell has his new boat, and I have promised to go and see it."

"And not you, Charlie?"—for I knew Charlie's interest in all the Ashleigh people was always keener than Alan's.

"Charlie was not invited," said Alan, almost hastily, but with a laugh. "Good-bye. I shall try to join you after the singing practice, but I may possibly not be in time."

So we answered his good-bye, and went on

together down the lane—I still wondering
why Charlie had not helped me in persuading Alan to come. The hedge-banks are so
rich in flowers now that it naturally took
us a long time to reach even the first
cottage in the village—old Burley's. He
was busy in his garden, and whilst I lingered upstairs with his sick daughter, Charlie
took the old man's spade and helped him.
From there we went with a message to
Mrs. Long, and I sat and bawled to her old
deaf mother, while Charlie chatted with
her, and tossed her baby; and I could not
help seeing with what immeasurable pride
she watched her baby pulling his short
bright curls. Surely how all our villagers
love him!

Then we went to the village shop, and
found old Rebecca sweeping and dusting it,
for a wonder. So Charlie took off his coat
and arranged the higher shelves for her,
then sat on the counter, making her laugh
heartily, while she weighed me some tea
for Ben, and a parcel of sweets he himself

wanted for some purpose. When we went on into Ben's room—the poor old pensioner who lodges with her—we found he wanted a letter written to his son in India, so Charlie promised to come back and write it, as soon as he had taken me to the church.

"You will wait here till I come for you, Hope," he said, when we had climbed the funny little hill on which the white church stands, and he was unlocking the heavy door for me.

"Yes—if you come before the practice is over."

"Of course I shall, because you will make the practice last till I come. We will not give Ben's son quite so long a letter as we generally do."

"You always *do* write such unconscionably long letters, Charlie," I observed, laying my wild flowers down on the collecting box inside the door.

"Only to you, my little Hope," he said ; and then he took both my hands in his, among the dim, high pews—which always seem to me built just on purpose for our old people to sleep in unobserved—and he looked into my eyes with something so strange and warm and tender in his own, that somehow his name came from my lips in a little cry of pleasure. And then I was so much ashamed—so wonderfully ashamed!

"Hope," he whispered, "do you never guess what I want to tell you, and have so often been upon the point of telling you? Do you never guess how hard it is to me *not* to tell my love how I love her?"

I wonder what any other girl would have said. I wonder—I wonder whether any other girl, as happy as I felt at that moment, would have hidden it as sillily as I hid it?

"Of course you love me, Charlie. Haven't you loved me ever since you took me for your little sister, in old days?"

"I loved you then, my dear one," he

said, and I scarcely knew his merry face
in its great earnestness, " but I never took
you for my little sister. I don't believe
even Alan ever called you so—*I* never did.
And now "—he paused for a moment, his
clasp of my hands growing tighter, his
eyes very grave and anxious—" and, now
I am a man, Hope, and I know exactly
what a man's heart craves for. Look
up and satisfy mine, darling; for all its
love and all its tenderness are yours."

I could have done it, oh ! so easily, so
easily, for had I not loved him as long as
I could remember him? But the words
would not frame themselves. I don't think
he minded, though. It was just as if he
could read them in my eyes.

" I am so poor, Hope," he said, " that
perhaps I ought not to have told you this ;
but I have such great confidence in a man's
strength and power to do what he may
need to do, that I ventured. If you say
no to me, it will not be because I am poor.
If—if you do not say *no* to me, Hope," he

added, his voice stirred with gladness, though still so very low, "I shall go now and make a good start—what courage I shall have for it!—and come back presently to beg your father to give his little girl to me. What will she herself say? What," he asked again presently, for I had not answered, because I had felt words so weak in this great joy of mine. "What will my darling tell me then?" he asked once more, while he raised both the hands he held, and pressed them to his lips.

Then I answered him, in a whisper which was all truth,

"I can but tell you one thing, Charlie. I have loved you dearly—I think I have loved you dearly as long as I have known you."

"What good, sweet words!" he cried, with a wonderful light within his eyes, and a happy smile upon his lips. "If you only knew——"

"I *do* know," I said, drawing my hands

from his warm clasp, "that it is time to practise. Please hurry the children in, Charlie."

They came clattering in, almost as soon as he had left me; and one or two of them laid down a few wild flowers upon my lap, or on the harmonium beside me, as a little offering. My one alto boy had brought a handful of red campion, and I remembered, as I thanked him, an old superstition among our people that if you put a campion blossom into your pocket, it will not die unless the person you love best is faithless to you. So, quite solemnly, while I told the children what hymn to find, and bade them put away the sweets which evidently Charlie had already distributed among them, I slipped one of the bright flowers into the pocket of my dress.

When we had played through all the hymns and chants for Sunday—not that it is ever much use, for our old clerk always sings everything in a different key, and almost as loudly as all of us put together,

and though Charlie and Alan always range
on our side to try to deaden it when they
are at home, even that makes it very little
less excruciating—I dismissed the children, but went on playing to myself in the
cool shadowy old church, just as I love to
do. And somehow I knew that, happy as
my thoughts were, there was no new-
ness in their joy; so could it be that I
have always known how dearly Charlie
loved me?

Just as I thought of him, dreamily
playing over the hymn we had practised
last, he came up the aisle, singing the
words to it softly as he came,

> "Nothing in my hand I bring,
> Simply to Thy cross I cling."

"I love that hymn," he said, in his
gentle way, as he closed the harmonium
for me; "and when I picture this last
day——"

"Hush!" I cried, for the words really
hurt me. "I am trying to forget that you
are going to-morrow. You say you love

this place, Charlie, and I know everyone here loves you, *yet* you leave it."

"Yes, and I am going to win *you* to leave it too, darling, while they all love you far, far better. I must gain money for our future, Hope."

"I do dislike money so."

"What a happy thing!" he said, with his bright smile. "I don't want you to love anything I cannot give you."

"I would so much rather be poor," I said, slipping my hand into his as we paused in the church-porch, "because if one is poor, one knows that whoever loves one loves one for oneself alone."

"How else could one be *loved* at all, you little wise logician?" he queried, keeping prisoner the hand I had given him; "wise, I declare, as the queen of Sheba herself!"

"How?" I asked sedately, feeling very glad indeed that Charlie did not know of that campion blossom in my pocket.

"Don't you remember how Solomon

himself 'learnt in her bright eyes that to
be blest is to be wise?' That, you see, is
wisdom's crown of wisdom. Ah! there's
Alan."

He was walking slowly up the churchyard, and he smiled as we came into sight,
and said something rather merrily about
being just in time. Yet, at that moment,
and for the very first time in my petted
life, there came a strange, heavy feeling in
my heart, and I suddenly learnt the meaning of a word I never understood before
—*solitariness.* A moment afterwards I
thought how absurd this was; yet it made
me go to meet Alan, as he came on alone,
and made me stand beside him while we
all loitered against the churchyard wall
for a few idle, restful minutes.

"I don't know what the new ferry-boat
may be like close, Alan," said I, trying to
make him talk, "but it looks very pretty
from here."

"Yes," he said; but I noticed that his
eyes never went beyond the churchyard.

The sunshine sparkled on the little river winding through the valley, and high above our heads a tiny lark practised a sweeter hymn than any we had been able to learn within the church to-day. It was an hour to enjoy indeed, as I said quietly to Alan.

But it was Charlie who answered so earnestly,

" And to remember."

" Charlie," I said in my irrelevant way; turning a little from them now and plucking a few blades of the spear grass from the wall, " I almost wonder you are not a clergyman, because it seems as if life were going to be so serious with you."

"Perhaps it is, dear," he answered me, just as he used to answer me when a child; "but still I don't regret that I am not a clergyman."

" He never regrets anything; does he, Alan?" I asked, passing him a little bunch of my wild flowers for his coat, and so at last making him speak to me; but it was not

quite in his usual tones, nor somehow
did the words seems quite like Alan's
words.

"No; he reminds me of that old fellow
in Ingoldsby who left in his will 'a horse-
hair shirt as good as new.' Charlie's
penances are no more severe."

"I have a theory, you know," said
Charlie, after a moment's pause, " that no
one can preach Christ who is not truly
Christ. How otherwise can He be mani-
fested to the world livingly and effective-
ly? *He also in us.* In our seeing and
hearing, in our living and loving, *He* hears
and sees, and lives and loves. It is a
grave responsibility for us all, how much
more for the preachers, Hope ?"

I pondered this a good deal, wondering
what papa would say; but I'm sure he
would puzzle me still more if he tried to
explain, and so I will wait till it gets
adjusted. I think we have an innate sense
of truth and right and goodness, far deeper
and stronger than we dream, by which

things *do* get ultimately sifted and sorted pretty justly.

Opposite us, as we leaned against the churchyard wall, they had lately put up a new head-stone, elaborately painted; and now, just simply to break our pause—because it did not seem exactly like our old happy easy pauses—I read the florid inscription aloud :—

" 'Until the day dawn and the shadows flee,
HERE
Rests the body of Susan McGhee.'

Susan left a poet friend behind her, didn't she, Alan? Could you manage as well for me ?—

Until the night end and the day doth begin,
HERE
Rests the body of idle Hope Wynne."

" Exactly the same would do for me," laughed Charlie, with a sly glance across at me.

" Until the night end and the day doth begin,
HERE
Rests the body of Charlie Mostyn.

The accent is beautiful. You cannot make it fit *you*, though, Alan, try as you will."

"Alan's can be far more poetical," I said, speaking randomly as usual, but with a shy involuntary touch upon one hand of his, as it lay on the wall, because I had looked into his face.

"Until the day dawn and the shadows take wing,
        HERE
    Rests the body of Alan Field*ing*."

Oh ! what nonsense we three often talk ! But I the worst of all. How can they— I mean how can Charlie—really care for me, when I have such a small, small mind ?

New Year's Eve, 1868.   *Nearly midnight.*

We have had just one of our merry New Year's Eves. It was actually hard to believe we were not children again, playing noisy games, and acting ridiculous charades ; joining the village children in their carols ; telling fireside stories ; and making even papa and mamma laugh and run. I could almost have fancied it that first New Year's holiday of all, when I so well remember Charlie, dressed in mamma's own dress and shawl and bonnet, paying her a ceremonious call. And she never knew him, though I am sure I half betrayed him by my irresistible titters in the distance. I'm sure when I put his little curls all under the bonnet cap, and parted his hair in the middle, it looked just like a girl's. If it had not been for the moustache, I believe he would have been ready to play just such a trick to-day. Yes, it was just like old times, and delightful indeed to have Charlie and Alan here for it. Papa hopes they will stay with us longer than they did in the Summer, because he says Charlie is always better here than in his office, and that Alan can just as well write about things to do from here as from his town lodgings. As for what *I* hope—oh! what joy it is to have them.

I wonder, oh! I wonder, what is com-

ing to us in this new year, for which I do
not and cannot care a bit just yet, though
it may give me opportunities for complet-
ing some of my life's unfinished tasks.

How the wind has risen! It is as if the
old year sighed and trembled, and could
not bear to go; and indeed I cannot bear
to lose it. I love it more than ever to-
night, as I suppose we always love what we
are forced to lose. How good it has been!
How much it has given me! And who is
to tell what this new strange year is
bringing, as it comes so fast and stormily
to meet me?

January 25th, 1869.

St. Paul's Day.—And how the old lines
rushed into my mind this morning, as I
looked out upon the heavy mist—

> " If the day of Paul be clear,
>   Then will betide a happy year."

I sang very loudly to keep that thought
away, for this is Charlie's birthday as well
as " the day of Paul," and I wanted it to

be very, very bright. And I found it so indeed. Misty and grey as it has been in reality, I'm sure the day will always be clear and shining in my memory—just as last night, I remember, when we stood in the garden, that dark cloud, that threatened to hide the moon, grew bright in passing over it, and made it more beautiful.

As I had worked Charley a pair of slippers (dark blue embroidery on buff leather), and as slippers are rather difficult to disguise, however carefully folded up, I held my hands behind me going downstairs, for fear of his meeting me and seeing it all in a minute. And, presently, I was very glad I had, for there he was at the foot of the stairs, waiting for me.

"You must guess," I said, stopping at a safe distance from him; for he was the worst guesser I ever knew, and I liked—I mean I did not dislike—to puzzle him.

But he did not attempt to guess; he seemed in far too great a hurry, and, as my hands were not forthcoming, he put his

arm round me just as I stood, and, somehow, all in a minute I found he was stronger than I had ever known him to be; and
then—in the next moment, and before I
could understand at all—we were in papa's
study, and he was looking at us in the
greatest surprise, with his dear old, ugly
felt hat at the very back of his head. And
Charlie—still with his arm round me, and
with a funny tremble in his dear, bright
voice—was begging papa to give him *me*
for a birthday present!

I don't think I heard anything quite
clearly and properly, but, I remember, how
very, very earnest Charlie looked while he
pleaded; and that when at last I saw the
gladness of his gratitude to papa, my eyes
filled with tears, only just because my own
happiness was so intense.

I remember papa's long, quiet kiss, and
how I seemed to understand his silence;
and so bent my head and folded my hands
involuntarily, while his gentle touch lay on
my head.

Then I just remember Charlie's one kiss, and nothing more, until I had told it all, myself, with my face hidden in mother's lap.

* * * * * *

It was this afternoon, in the firelight. We—Charlie and I—were just wondering where Alan had been ever since breakfast, when he came in. Charlie rose to meet him, while I still sat in my low seat upon the rug; and looking round, saw, while Charlie spoke, how the firelight darted up to the two faces—one so happy, and the other, just then, so very grave.

"I guessed this, Hope,"—Alan was speaking to me now, and his voice sounded strangely calm and low after those exultant tones of Charlie's; and the hand he gave me felt unsteady, as well as so very cold,—"I have expected him to tell me this. Your happiness I love to think of, Hope; and as for his—I have little need to wish him many happy returns of such a day as this. There can be but one in a man's life."

"Oh! Alan," I cried, laying my other hand on his, and all my heart seemed to come into my eyes as I looked into his tired face, "will it not bring us *all* nearer to each other? I—I cannot bear a separation."

"Dear," he said, with a sudden change in his voice, and just a hurried pushing of the hair from his temples, "nothing can separate us now—I believe. What was it that made your eyes sadden on such a happy day as this? Charlie," he added, turning suddenly away from me, "Charlie, dear fellow, I have not half wished you joy."

But Charlie—what had he, too, seen in Alan's face to move him so?—Charlie sat at the table now, far out of the firelight, with his face hidden on his folded arms.

February 17th, 1869.

Alan left us to-day, but, to my joy,

Charlie stays a little longer. He every day seems to get more anxious about his prospects. He must earn now, he says, enough to give me everything I can enjoy. As if I needed much more than his love and care and company! Daily we discuss plans and projects of every kind, impossible as well as possible; but we never seem to reach any definite conclusion. Papa has always advised Charlie to stick to his profession, but it seems that instead of gaining he has been losing by it from the beginning, so even papa begins to acknowledge that it is no use thinking of that. Sometimes he tries to help us, and often now Allan has a suggestion to make, strange to say, for Charlie—apart from himself. But energetically as Charlie always enters into every fresh plan, none as yet has been a practicable one.

And it is so sad to watch both him and Alan bear every fresh disappointment. What *will* they do!

"Perhaps we think too much about it,"

Alan said to me this morning, as we two stood in the old porch, just before the time came for his good-bye. " We look on it as a matter of such engrossing import-ance, to carve our own destinies; and yet, as Prospero says, you know, we are only ' of such stuff as dreams are made of, and our little life is rounded with a sleep !' "

" Hush, Alan, please!" I cried, noticing how almost stern his young face looked against the frosty ivy leaves.

" It will be all well at last," he said, with a change of tone, just as if he had been speaking before on a different subject altogether. " Charlie will get on famously, Hope, and not stay long away from you; while you—dear little Hope, ' for you each evening hath its shining star, and every Sabbath day its golden sun !' "

" And you, Alan ?" I whispered.

" I have a—hope of my own too," he answered, just in his usual way. " My dear, without faith and hope of *some* kind, what should we any of us be ?"

By this time they had all found us, and in five minutes more Alan had waved his handkerchief to us for the last time, as we all stood at the garden gate ; and Charlie had driven him out of sight on the Gloucester Road.

"I am glad Charlie insisted on driving him into Gloucester," papa said. "They are all right while they are together ; eh, Hope ?"

"Yes," I said, but I was only thinking how this was a little foretaste of the parting that has to come.

"Best of all when they are together," papa went on, in his absent, dreamy way, while we still leaned over the gate, looking along the unfrequented road. "I remember that Montaigne ranks friendship higher, and more important and engrossing than love."

*   *   *   *   *   *

How long will Charlie be ?
Oh ! how I dislike Montaigne.

March 10*th*, 1869.

Charlie's last day here is over now. To-morrow he goes back to work. This farewell will be terrible, I fear; he has been so long with us this time, and he and I have been so entirely all in all to each other. But he is right, of course. It is time that he should go.

Sometimes now the old shadow lies for quite a long time in his eyes, and I seem to lose all my happiness in a minute. Then I know that I would rather part from him—ay, even for years—than not lighten for him this great care for our future.

" I am sure you think me a changeable fellow, Hope," he said to me this morning, after he had had a long and serious discussion with papa; " but there is *one* thing in which I can never know a moment's change. Is it as altogether impossible that *you* will change in your love for me, dearest ?"

" *Your* love will be shared by work, and

change, and travel, Charlie," I said, fighting with the tears that were so near my eyes all day; "while mine will be—I think it will be my whole life here, till——Oh! my love, you will come back to me?"

I don't know what he said in answer to that sudden, irrepressible cry of mine, but I was so much, much happier after he had said it.

*   *   *   *   *   *

March 11th, 1869.

He has gone! Every leaf and flower in the garden seems to have a voice, and is saying that to me. Every dumb, inanimate object in the old house seems to know and tell me afresh that he is gone. There is no spot where I do not miss him; there is no task which will take my thoughts from him. I cannot speak to anyone, because my voice is full of tears.

And yet this must not be. I told him I would think of nothing but his coming back again. I remember telling him that, and he never knew how hard it was to say. It was at that last moment. I had watched him driven out of sight along the road, just as I had watched Alan; and I was trying to bear it quietly, and had my hands very tight upon the gate, and my face hidden in them; when he came running back, and caught me in his arms, and kissed me once again, and told me——

Oh! it was all worse than ever that last time.

I wonder whether it could be really *kind* to that little family in Bethany to bring back the brother, after that bitterness of parting and death was past—for had it not all to come again?

May 20th, 1869.

For the last few days I have had such strange, excited letters from Charlie.

" Be glad with me, dear love, for at last I see my way to perfect happiness, and even to great wealth, for you and me.

Hope, darling, I shall soon come to fetch you to a beautiful home in the richest and loveliest country in the world."

That was in his first letter, and the others have told me very little more; except that I can read in every line his unmeasured content in this new project, and—and I try so hard to understand it, and to have faith in it, as he has.

We have been all morning reading the pamphlets Charlie has sent us. Father looked very heavy-hearted over them, and I saw tears in mother's eyes (for they both love Charlie and Alan just as if they were my real brothers). Each page took me a long, long time to read, for through my tears I could scarcely distinguish the words. I only knew that they all seemed to say just one thing—only one—that Charlie was going away; that presently half the wide world would be between us, and that all my longing and all my love were powerless to keep him. Yet it is chiefly for my sake that he goes, to make a home of ease and luxury, he says, for me. I don't want ease and luxury—I want Charlie. Oh! how pitiful it is! This new country is so far away, and life and health are so un-· certain.

But there—I will *not* look at it so drearily. I correct myself a hundred times a day, but even yet I cannot summon courage to write to Charlie cheerily, as I ought to do; and I will write to him in no other way.

I wonder what Alan thinks of this scheme. He was always so much more deliberate than Charlie. Yet he would have even greater temptations to join this emigrant expedition, for not only (like Charlie) has he no relative in the old country, but he has even no profession, and no tie —but how silly it would be to call myself *a tie* to keep Charlie here, when it is partly for my sake he goes! Father thinks Alan will be too sceptical to join, but mother fancies they will go together. I think so too, they are such true friends.

May 22, 1869.

I have read the pamphlets again to-day, slowly and carefully, and without letting my tears blind me, for I had made up my mind to search for all the good that Charlie saw, and to try to write to him of only *that*. And it was not hard to find it, for each book is filled with glowing accounts of that rich and beautiful country, which they may well call the Emigrants' *El Dorado*. " Wealth and independence—indeed affluence—are to be acquired there in a very few years, and the emigrants still will only be at the distance of a pleasant trip from their old familiar scenes."

The vast tract of this highly-favoured land (I am quoting now from books Charlie sent me, telling of this Vyse grant to which he intends to go) is distant only seventeen days by steamer from England, and is the most fertile and healthy country in the world. In a few years it will form the most successful settlement known, the interests of

the emigrants being carefully looked after
by the Company, where multitudes, besides
Anthony Trollope, "will find the Elysium
of the Tropics, the one true Utopia of the
Caribbean Sea, the Transatlantic Eden."
One acre in Venezuelan Guayana is equal
to thirty in England. The year is one
continuous Spring, and this country is the
garden spot of the world.

When I read these things, I ought of
course to feel all Charlie's hopes and anticipations; even his gratitude that, as he
says, this scheme has so providentially been
brought just now under his notice. So I
will read no more to-day, for fear of the
old mistrust and fear creeping back so
icily into my heart. Because is it not
true that nearly all things—like Yamen—
have two aspects, one for the eyes of Hope,
the other for the eyes of Fear?

May 28, 1869.

Charlie writes now in the highest
spirits.

So high his hopes have grown, that mine are following them, though of course far more feebly and doubtingly.

I wish I knew exactly what Alan thinks of this great enterprise. Charlie jestingly says that one assurance in Mrs. Matherson's letters is sure to prove irresistible with Alan. It is that "in this wonderful country the emigrant can enjoy daily all the year round the *aldermanic* luxury of turtle soup." Think of that influencing either Charlie or Alan!

But with real pleasure I have read the Code of Laws drawn up, evidently with such wise care and forethought, for the Mathersonville Colony, by the benevolent lady who encourages the emigrants—for I must own with Charlie that she *is* kind and benevolent, though it is through her that he and I are to be separated for a time. It makes me almost glad and happy to remember these laws. I think I would like to copy one or two. This is the first, and it may well head the thirty-three, good as they all are :—

"That the Divine Creator be acknowledged as the Supreme Author, Legislator, Guide, and Protector of the people."

And the last paragraph in this good and wise little book is this :—

"Finally, knowing our frailty as human beings, and considering that without a blessing from on high all man's efforts must be vain, we humbly and reverently place these our feeble laws of guidance, with our whole trust and confidence in Him, the great Judge and Ruler of the universe, who alone can direct us aright, make us happy, and protect us, and on whose mighty arm we lean for support in this new and adventurous undertaking we have commenced. Amen."

Surely those words ought to give me courage. So I close the books Charlie sent me, and will try to be patient.

Oh, suppose I didn't know that while *we* would do ever so much for those we love there is a tenderness infinitely—infinitely—beyond the tenderness of our human hearts. But—I think I cannot write any more until that terrible good-bye is over.

PART II.

FROM CHARLIE MOSTYN'S DIARY.

" 'Tis true, 'tis pity."
SHAKESPEARE.

July 24th, 1869.

AT last I may write that all is settled. Alan has to-day gone to obtain his land warrant. Even *his* caution and scepticism are vanquished now, and he is almost as excited as myself over this splendid undertaking.

"Charlie, you are fatally credulous," he used to say; but he sees now that I had no occasion to be anything *but* credulous, and he is grateful to me for holding on to the scheme so steadily as to take him with me, past all his fears and scruples. How he ever could, for a moment, have hesitated over this enterprise, is unaccountable to me. There we were, two months ago, staring blankly into the future, and seeing no prospect of ever winning more than a bare subsistence. I struggling in vain to live upon my profession, without a client or a patron; and Alan plodding without heart after every scheme he heard of; all his old hopes and ambitions trampled into dust.

But, thank God, that is over now; and to-day the seal is to be put to the deed which will soon make us wealthy, healthy men; and give us homes of our own, where there will be no need for us to grind and save; suppressing every manly wish and natural longing. Above them all, what a home mine shall be! With Hope's sweet little figure brightening it, and her happy voice as free from every note of sorrow as a bird's.

What happy words she said, dear Hope, when, in our favourite spot in the old study window at the vicarage, I pictured to her the home I am going out to make for my wife! Even her father was proud and pleased, and perhaps, poor fellow, he regrets the many years he has worked in that little parish, only to be able even now barely to provide for his wife, and the one pet girl whom he will spare to me when, in two years' time, I come home a rich and prosperous man, to fetch her to her beautiful new home.

Poor Alan has no such aim for which to leave England, and so it was natural, perhaps, that he should take so long to decide upon a step over which *I* could not long pause.

Just as I wrote that, Alan came in and read it over my shoulder—for this diary is as familiar to him as to me.

"I'm afraid my caution and scepticism are not quite all vanquished, as you assert," he said, rather sadly, as he turned to the window. "I wish to heaven they were—as we *are* going."

"They are dying rapidly, if not already dead, old fellow. Just remember what we are, Alan, landed proprietors in the richest and most beautiful country in the world."

I had risen in my enthusiasm, and stood now laughing into Alan's face, with my hands on his shoulders. We are as nearly of a height as possible, and even alike in other respects too, though there is not the frailest tie of kindred between us. But often, when I look into Alan's face, I wish that my own had its strength; for I can sometimes feel my colour change so oddly. Just as if I were a girl, I cannot help flushing at a friendly glance or touch, and paling over a disappointment or word of coldness. And at such times, I sometimes see a look exchanged, which tells me that those who have known my parents remember something which excuses me.

But all this weakness has been forgotten lately, in the delightful excitement of preparing for my new career, whose happiness now is increased tenfold, because I and my old friend are to be together still.

" You have your land-warrant *now*, Alan ?"

"Yes, I have made my going certain now," said Alan, with a note of sadness in his voice. But presently he seemed to try to shake it off, and spoke more easily. "Charlie, I want you to come and see Colonel Boyd. As he is to be leader to the party sailing in July, it would be well, I think, for us to have a talk with him. Mrs. Matherson has given me his address."

I assented to this arrangement willingly enough, even eagerly, for I had often wished for a personal knowledge of the gentleman who was to "lead" our expedition. So we have decided to go this afternoon. I am so glad Alan has his land-warrant. He now, like myself, will be a citizen on landing ; will not pay taxes; is entitled to a share of the stock of the Company, and will participate in all their rights, privileges, benefits, immunities and profits. No wonder one of Mrs. Matherson's pamphlets asserts that "this opportunity is the tide in the affairs of men which, taken at the flood, leads on to fortune."

*   *   *   *   *   *

I am very glad we paid that visit to Colonel Boyd to-day ; his confidence (though it made no change in *my* feelings) had, I could see, a great effect upon Alan ; not one word has he uttered since of his old qualms or doubts. He is now as certain as I am that we have found exactly the opportunity we needed—a brighter future even than we used to picture, as boys, in our wildest and happiest day-dreams. How could he now think other-wise, even though he has doubted hitherto? Colonel Boyd is a man past middle age, and has a wife and eight children, yet he goes out in the fullest certainty of prospering in Venezuelan Guayana, with a rapidity which no settler on English ground can conceive. As Alan so truly says, the very fact of this

thoughtful, experienced soldier sinking
all the money he possesses, and taking
such a family out, scatters all doubts more
effectually than a dozen pamphlets could.
Colonel Boyd behaved more like a boy
than either of us, while he answered Alan's
polite and sceptical request as to his motive
for choosing to emigrate to Venezuelan
Guayana.

"Motive?" he answered, laughing. "I
have a hundred motives. I can see, from
the Mathersons' books and letters, that
no place in the world could suit me so
well. First, it requires less capital than
any of the colonies; then the climate is
the very one for an officer who has spent
years in India, it being equal to the Cape,
the best climate in the world. Then,
from the absence of frost and snow, we
can carry on agricultural operations all
the year round, and the fertility of the soil
yields every year three crops of cotton
(quite the most profitable sort of farming)
as well as all sorts of European cereals.

Eight feet deep, it is the richest virgin soil, so that we do not need that scientific knowledge of farming which is necessary in England and Canada, and which I myself, as a military man, of course, have had no opportunity of acquiring. As Mrs. Matherson's pamphlet says, 'the country only wants earth-subduing man to make it the Garden of Plenty.' In such a climate men must live luxuriously. And last, though not least," he added, laughing again, "in Mathersonville we shall need no revolvers. In short, I believe this to be the grandest project in the way of emigration which the world has ever known, and anyone insane enough to prefer going to the British Colonies, actually *deserves* the comparative ruin with which he would assuredly meet. Then the laws of the Company are liberal and well administered; religion is entirely free from all sectarianism; schools are supported, teachers salaried, the Sabbath strictly observed, and worship performed by our own ministers. One thing I notice, that, though all roads are open to political position, only a native or a child born on the land can be President of the Republic; but, as Mrs. Matherson says, ' *this item should not deter emigration.*' "

Colonel Boyd told us he was purchasing seeds then, as his outfit was already complete. All he considers necessary for each of us to take is a tent, a hammock, a rod and tackle, and a rifle; a plough, a harrow, two spades, two picks, two axes, a tool-box, half a dozen flannel shirts, and a few holland suits.

Alan, I could see, was taking mental notes of all he said, and eventually we parted like old friends—as we shall soon feel in our new homes.

So now Alan and I have only our own personal preparations to make. We possess our land-warrants, which are only issued by Mrs. Matherson's Company, and her clerk went with us to the Venezuelan Consul, who signed and put on them the seal of the Republic, then gave us our passports.

At Bolivar each emigrant must show this land-warrant to the Governor, who will *viser* it, and place the seal of the state of Guayana upon it, giving us then our citizenship. After that we select the site of our land on the Vyse Grant, and mark the boundaries; for the Company has agents at Bolivar and every port in the Orinoco, as well as at Trinidad.

Mrs. Matherson (she seems to act in this matter much more than her husband does, so I daresay she is much more energetic and benevolent, and has the well-being of the Company more at heart) has carefully calculated the expenses of the journey, and sent us her list (Alan is now posting her the stamps which she reminds us we have omitted to return for pamphlets, &c., since our last payment). I daresay it will come within the sum we fancied, though if, as Alan suspects, it goes beyond, we shall still be able to meet it. I am

drawing the whole of my principal to in-
vest and take, and it is plenty to start us
both (for Alan's is smaller still) on this
high road to wealth.

The closing words of Mrs. Matherson's
last letter run in my head deliciously—
" There is every chance for men who care
to get rich to do so in that fair land ; and
every inducement for farming on those
splendid lands." And then I like to remind Alan how very excellent and thoughtful are all the regulations for our spirited
and united little band ; and for the guiding
and governing of that greater colony
which we go to join in Mathersonville.
Who but a kind, large-hearted woman
would have so carefully compiled that code
of laws—laws of justice, honour, and religion—and so wisely ordered the adminis-
tration of general business affairs ? Even
the electing of mayor and council (twelve
men), police and harbour-master—all by
the forethought of our wise Lady Promoter.
How can we help, under her rule, enjoying

the peace and harmony which, as she herself says, are so essential to the welfare of
the colony? What a power of helping
their fellow-countrymen has this possession given to the Mathersons!

Alan and I have decided to join our
funds, and purchase twelve hundred and
eighty acres of the new rich land, and
even this (with also a share of stock in the
Company) will only cost us two hundred
pounds. Think of it! And of its being
land producing cotton, sugar, coffee, cocoa,
corn, rice, tapioca, sago, wheat, barley, and
oats; fruits of every kind; drugs of every
kind; indigo and dye logwoods of every
kind, with plenty of other valuable roots
still unknown in Europe! Then its forest
timber is magnificent, while the plains are
filled with herds of oxen, horses, mules,
goats, and deer. Did not Humboldt pro-
nounce this country to be "the garden
spot of the world?" Our money, both for
the land and our passage, is to be paid at
the Matherson's office here, so that will

save us trouble. I am going to take two lads—strong Gloucestershire lads, whom I knew in the old Vicarage days—and Alan takes a vigorous young fellow who for years has been looking out for an opportunity of emigrating. That will be enough, because we shall both work so hard ourselves during the few years which the Mathersons assure us is all the time that is needed to acquire affluence in Mathersonville. I never cease to feel thankful that we heard of this scheme in time! We might have rusted on here for twenty years, without advancing as we shall advance in twenty weeks out there. Think of there being scarcely a couple of inhabitants to a square league, in the most fertile and healthy country in the world! What a field for us active fellows!

July 28th, 1869.

We have completed our preparations now, and leave for Gloucestershire tomorrow morning. I never hear a sign of

wavering and suspicion from Alan now.
He is as thoroughly convinced as I am
that we are doing the wisest thing in the
world ; and that we have need to be grateful all our lives to Mrs. Matherson. Still,
perhaps Alan is happier and more at ease
for having well investigated the matter
first.   As Mrs. Matherson herself says,
in one of her letters, " There is nothing
like investigation, for one's comfort in mat-
ters of *this* kind."

We have our coupons and passports, and
we have each a copy of a code of laws for
the Mathersonville Settlement, to which
we have signed our names as entirely ap-
proving them.   How could we do otherwise, when they are so wisely framed ?   It
is strange that even yet we have none of
us seen the president of the company—Mr.
Matherson.   Some of our letters come
from him, and some from his wife, but, as
Alan soon found out, the writing is the
same in each.   We, the pioneer party, are
to sail next month, with Mrs. Matherson

herself,—sixty-five of us. All, except Colonel
Boyd's family, Alan, myself, and two more,
being artizans and labouring men ; many
of them with wives and families.

This pioneer party was to have left
England in June, but, of course, in such
an undertaking delay is often unavoidable.
We think it wiser to go in a sailing vessel,
as steamers are so expensive, else it is only
seventeen days' steam from London to
Bolivar. Why, my journey home, presently, when I come to fetch Hope, will be
nothing ! Besides, as Colonel Boyd has
been made captain-superintendent and
major of the settlement for two years, *he*
would, in any case, feel pledged in honour
to go out with Mrs. Matherson and her
party ; to assist her in the management of
the emigrants on board ship.

I suppose the vessel will be off Gravesend
in a week or ten days. Most of those days
we may spend at Ashleigh. A whole week
with Hope !

Is it not Longfellow who says, somewhere, "Go forth into the shadowy future without fear, and with a manly heart!"

August 8th, 1869.

Even in the glorious future which we expect, can any week be happier than this which I have just spent with Hope, among those lovely scenes which time has made so familiar to me, and love has made so dear? What strength this farewell visit to the home of our orphan boyhood, has given to both Alan and me.

Now we are back in our London lodgings, waiting for our summons to join the emigrants. We have nothing more to do, and this first day has dragged a little, in spite of my exuberant anticipations and Alan's serene content. What is Hope doing now, while the sun sets behind the valley where we sat and promised——Now Alan proposes a walk. Even in the London streets, we can talk of that glorious country in which we shall be walking in a few weeks' time.

August 12th, 1869.

We are still waiting for a vessel, but we are to sail from Hamburg. Mrs. Matherson says the emigration commissioners have advised it, saying that even if the vessel is only one half-inch smaller than the regulation act requires, there will be trouble; and she would in that case lose her security of two thousand five hundred pounds. So it is considerate of the commissioners to have advised her to take her party to Hamburg. But some of the better sort of emigrants have already gone by steamer, in preference to waiting for a sailing vessel.

Hamburg, September 25th, 1869.

We have already waited more than six weeks for a ship, while none of us know any real reason for the delay. First the doubt is whether the vessel is large enough, according to the emigration act (she is three hundred and ninety tons, and we are sixty-nine people). Then we hear that the

shipping firm requires guarantees, and that
Mrs. Matherson has not paid up the sum
required by the owners; and so there is a
prospect of the arrangement even now being cancelled.   Colonel Boyd writes to us
in the greatest anxiety, and has, in despair,
tried his influence with the owners of this
ship—which is the third which has been promised us.   He wishes us to make up among
ourselves the sum Mrs. Matherson will not
pay, that we may have the ship.   "For if
we do not go at once," he writes, "I, at
any rate, shall be stranded."   I am sorry
for Mrs. Matherson, but Alan has some-
what changed in his feelings towards her
and her husband.   When we are once on
board, we shall judge with less prejudice,
and, no doubt, she will be able to explain
this delay.

Our resources are fast dwindling, through
our protracted stay in this town.   Boyd
says, if it had not been that a woman
managed the affair, there would have been
a guarantee for the ship sailing on a cer-

tain day, or, in the event of its not doing
so, the passengers would have been main-
tained at the owner's expense. No such
arrangement was made, though, and we
stay on, exhausting our funds, and sinking into real despair. It is serious for us
all, but most so for Colonel Boyd, with his
large family, and I recall how cheerfully
he laid out his ready money, expecting to
be on his own land almost by this time.

October 6th, 1869.

At last we are under weigh. I have
made no entry in my diary through those
wasted weeks in Hamburg, for it has been
a time of real hardship to us all. Alan
says he is quite sure now that the motive
for our meeting the ship in Hamburg, was
to prevent the emigration commissioners
discovering imposition in the undertaking.
This is, of course, only a suspicion of
Alan's; but, at any rate, Mrs. Matherson
never appeared, and we have left England
without her. Cleverly as everything has

been arranged in writing, I fancy Colonel
Boyd may be right when he says he is
sure now that Mrs. Matherson had never
intended to come.

We are fairly off now. No turning back
for any of us, for all we possess is either
on this ship, or waiting for us in the new
country—a wonderful country of wealth
and beauty, as I remind myself a hundred
times a day.

Can Hope guess how I long for one
word? Or how immense the distance seems
between us?

Bolivar, November 26th, 1869.

For three days we stayed on board;
then landed our luggage here; and
to-night Alan and I have even found a
bedroom, obtainable, after waiting several
days for it. We have engaged a boat (for
£16) to take us to Caura. The assistance
promised us by the Company is not forthcoming, and our party could not go on,
but that the president has supplied them,

not only with boats, but with three months' provisions too.

December 8th, 1869.

Yesterday the first boats left for Caura, Colonel Boyd and his party leading the way. To-day Alan and I started, with our two dogs, my two boys, and Alan's facto-tum.

About midday (we had started soon after six) we passed all the other boats, except Boyd's. We have rough work and rough fare, but the sailors are civil, and the river banks seem fertile. We ran aground two or three times, and met plenty of crocodiles. We sleep on shore to-night.

December 14th, 1869.

To-day we have a better wind, and the mountains are in sight, but the worst part of the river has yet to be navigated. The current is so strong we have to travel close to the bank, pushing with poles and pulling by the bushes, while even then our boats are continually turning round. I have not had much sleep on the river (not that that is a very new thing for me, even without mosquitoes), but only once have we been wet through by the sharp and sudden rain.

Yesterday all the boats came up together, and Alan and I spoke to Colonel Boyd for the first time since we left Bolivar. I shot three wild duck, but we could not get them, on account of the current. It is terribly hot, and we have no awning, but Alan and I had some sport. Among other "game," we shot three alligators, for they come in swarms about us. I caught a cat-fish of about twenty pounds, and Alan hooked a monster which broke his line. It is night now, and he is lying on his back humming "Home, sweet home." No use my trying to sleep, for the mosquitoes would not let me, so I write on, and being rather afraid of trusting myself to join Alan's song, I only lay down my pen just to remind myself to what a beautiful country we are bound, and how easy it will be to make a " home" there.

Tuesday, Dec. 19.

We are still wet and uncomfortable from our drenching yesterday, but the scenery is less gloomy, and I shot two more wild duck, though we could not get at them. Alan brought down four American snipe, which were famous eating. We are staying on shore to-day to make a covering for our boat, as the rain is constant now.

While I am working hard, there lies all the time, below all I do and say, the memory of Christmas time at home, and Hope —ah, it is far, far better not to think of her, not even to think of *home* (such an immeasurable distance away as it seems!) just now, except in my prayers. It will need all the strength we have to face our future here. Alan has just been reading a psalm to us, then we sang an old hymn which we all knew, and perhaps He to whom we sang it did not mind that our voices had so little power, and no spirit in them. My two lads require constant cheering and encouragement, and I cannot give it them now, for the mosquitoes seem to have possession of me. Alan is always brave and hopeful, and tries his best to stay this growth of a great disheartenment among the people. Those canoemen, to whom our provisions were confided by the president, have stolen them all.

Dec. 21, 1869.

This morning one of the Englishmen's wives threw herself into the river. Later on, a horrible fight took place, and neither Alan nor I could separate the men. I don't think I ever before saw women stand by at such a scene, and gaze in utter apathy. I tremble to think how hard (even if possible) it will be to re-unite us, after the spirit of discord has once broken out amongst us.

Dec. 23, 1869.

Another fight to-day. And two of the

babies are ill. The rapid and rushing currents make it almost impossible for us to make any head. One of the sick babies died to-night.

Christmas Day.

Travelling very slowly, and feeling very stiff and cramped from the crushing in our small canoe. I shot a Muscovy duck, and we had a good dinner. One of my boys down with fever. I gave him tea and quinine, wrapped him up in a blanket, and made him smile a little at his position. I'm terribly afraid that Alan suffers even more than I do, from the total lack of rest, for he has not been used to so little sleep, as I. The river banks are wooded down to the water's edge, and we pass but few spots where it is possible to land at all. The rain continues, but we are nearing our destination now—thank God!—and once more I cannot help feeling hopeful. True, the scenery is very disappointing, but I would not mind that, if only I could pre-

vent the mosquitoes biting me all night,
and the sandflies all day, as well as the
enormous ants which come in clouds from
the river banks. We are all huddled
together with the dogs in this small canoe,
and we can make no advance at all except
by pulling with all our strength (and that
means so sadly little now) by the bushes
which grow down to the water. Still, as
I said, we are not far from our destination
now, though when I remind Alan of that
he only mutters that "time is distance."
Certainly we can only make two or three
miles in a day, against the wind and current. We have taken down our mast, of
course. Whatever we kill only keeps
good for a couple of hours, the heat is so
intense ; and most of our party have only
rice and beans to live on now.

I looked up then, just to catch Alan
standing opposite me, in a long, miserable
gaze. I know why—I am getting very
thin and exhausted by this constant restlessness (to help the mosquitoes in their

marauding, there comes now a beetle, out
of the palm-leaves which we use to keep
our property dry in the canoe), and he
must be very tired of seeing me so. I'm
glad to rise and join him, for I had been
thinking far too deeply of the old Vicarage,
in its Christmas warmth and love; and recalling how, for eleven years, we have all
spent this time happily together.   We read
a chapter in St. John, and sang a few old
carols, which the boys remembered, and
some of the others joined us.   One or two,
who had sat sulkily apart at first, or laughed,
gradually came, one by one, to listen, or to
help us.

To-night, as Alan and I went among
the emigrants, we saw misery enough to
make the strongest of us like a child.   It
is impossible to describe the suffering of
he children from the bites of these venomous insects, which are all we see of living
creatures—except reptiles.

We suffer a good deal from hunger now,
and have an intense longing for meat which

is unattainable. Awake all night, but I am getting wearily used to that. For hours to-night Alan and I have sat talking of the old Christmas days.

December 27th, 1869.

We had hoped to be at our destination to-day, but the wind and the current are too much against us. Alan, in his grave, sad way, tells me (for I am almost entirely disabled from moving by the bites of the beetles and mosquitoes) that there is a terrible spirit of atheism creeping in among the people. I have not left our boat to-day, for one of the sailors fell ill, and I am trying to do something for him. Both my lads are suffering, but they bear up pretty bravely yet.

December 29th, 1869.

Yesterday afternoon we reached our destination.

What can I say?

At first—ay, and for long minutes—we stood—*paralysed*. Then, just for one moment, Alan and I looked into each other's eyes; and though I saw the misery of his heart, he answered my look with a touch upon my hand which I seemed to understand. And then at once, without a word or another glance, we began our work. This spot is a dense forest, through which we have to cut our way, step by step, even before we can land our luggage. They tell us the prairie ground is only reached through *twelve miles* of this bush, infested by a very venomous tirantula as large as a man's hand, and from whose bite the natives say there is no cure. Have I written it plainly—this awful truth, which is another name for ruin and death? The land is a dense, uncleared, tropical forest, liable to be overflowed during the wet season. Not a tree has been cut, not a swamp drained, nor a hut built. And the sickly, half-dead remnants of another party of emigrants (who came out four years ago) are working still hopelessly and uselessly, like men in a miserable dream.

We have just cleared bare room for
our tent, and killed five tirantulas. One
of my boys is totally unable to work.
Alan's young fellow moves his limbs like
an old man of eighty. We can only see
a few yards beyond us. I dare not face
Colonel Boyd, his trouble must be so immense—so far beyond the power of words
to reach. The women are sobbing at their
work, and now and then there comes from
a man's lips a moan which it is terrible to
hear. Mrs. Matherson's name is mutter-
ed, now and then, as a curse amongst us.

This evening Colonel Boyd raised his
head from his work one minute, as I came
up to him, and I never saw such a face of
misery in my life. " I am ruined," he
said simply ; but no more words were
needed. Two of his children are very ill.
I was fortunately able to relieve the boy a
little.

" *Now*," Alan said, entering our tent
just as I wrote, " I can understand exactly
what it would be to wake and feel my

coffin round me, knowing I had been
buried before my time. Charlie, speak!
Say something—*anything*—about the ruin
brought upon us by that fiend of a woman,
who should be made to answer for this
murder, if—if I could ever reach her. But
she knew she was safe. She knew that
not one of her poor dupes could live to
tell the world of her wholesale slaugh-
ter——What's the matter? *I'm* not faint
or ill, old fellow. Please God *that* trouble
shall not be laid upon you."

Upon *me!* It is always of some one
else that Alan thinks!

January 2nd, 1870. *Sunday.*

It has been impossible to write each
day. Not one of us yesterday dared to
breathe the familiar wish, " A happy new
year." Would anyone utter such a wish
to a condemned man as he mounted the
scaffold? *A happy new year!* Happy!
when we have spent all we have, as well
as all the hope and trust a man *can* have,

in hastening to ruin, disease, and death! How very, very far away the old home seems. Our eyes—so always heavy and weary now—can never rest again upon the dear, dear home!

Alan, sitting near me, is wondering—in a strange, vague, sceptical way which is sadly growing upon him—why we didn't break stones at home. With a ghost of a smile, I tell him there were no pumpkins there.

Boyd read us part of the service this morning, but very few cared to listen; and the cries of pain and rage and mourning broke every moment upon the tender, patient words.

This evening there was an alarming outbreak; fanatics and roughs at last gave free vent to their madness of despair, and we have been for four hours trying to quell it. Two more of the men are down with fever and ague. Alan is growing very weak, for want of meat, which we never taste.

January 3rd, 1870.

We are ceaselessly at work, felling the timber, which is hard almost as iron; and I cannot help recalling the mockery of that one statement in those mocking laws, that "permission to cut the timber can be granted solely by the Captain Superintendent, Mayor and Council." The underwood is dense and thick and thorny, and is filled with these ants, which bite so terribly. We can only hope to clear sufficient for every head of a family to have one quarter of an acre, on which to grow pumpkins for bare subsistence. This is our glorious home, in "the garden spot of the world!" Four men, one woman, and three children are laid up to-day. Alan asks what we are to do in the rainy season. The fever will have its own way then, for not one breath of fresh air can possibly reach us. The atmosphere is heavy with damp, and everything we possess is mouldy and mildewed. We are ourselves saturated with perspiration from morning till evening, yet even in all this heat we must not cease chopping and lugging, for if we are to live we must get daylight into the place, and have space to breathe and move. Scarcely a word is spoken among us, as we work doggedly on; only every downcast face tells its own tale of passion and despair.

January 4th, 1870.

Men, women, and children are falling off, and not merely as they did at first, one by one. Some people at Bolivar told us doggedly we should die here, but how little we thought their words would so soon and fatally come true! If, by parting with every farthing I possess, I could go with Alan out of this fearful country, how grateful I should be! If only the remnant of my little fortune would hire us something to free us from this living death! * * * When I had written that idea, which had been floating shapelessly for days in my weak, dazed brain, I went to Alan's ham-

G 2

mock to tell him; yet, when he started up with such a perfect fever in his eyes, I was terrified by what I had done.

The rain lies in a pool at the bottom of his hammock. Of course we have not slept out of our clothes since we left Bolivar.

"Those who stay in this place," I said to Colonel Boyd to-day, "*must* die."

"And can we care now," he answered, "how soon?"

Perhaps to Alan, as well as to myself, there had come before to-night a faint thought of the possibility of getting away, but it had never been uttered till I roused him now. At last, when his mind had grasped my meaning, and I had seen just once again for a moment the smile I never thought to see upon his face again, he put his weak arms round me, without any shame, man as he was, and then—we neither of us could help it—we both cried like children.

January 5th, 1870.

We all work on—all that death leaves,

and disease does not disable—in the same dogged manner, while abject despair is written on every face. Alan and I are dreaming now over our new project. If it might only be possible! How I wish the money were *his* instead of mine, then he would be unreserved with me in his plans and proposals. Boyd's youngest child died to-day. Very heavy rains; bedding and everything soaked. To-night one of the men suddenly threw down his axe, raised his hands to his head with a terrible shriek, and rushed into the depths of the forest—a raving lunatic.

Things look worse every day, yet has not everything connected with this fatal expedition gone wrong from the very beginning? To-day work seems suspended; quite half of the people are laid up, and the rest look worn and haggard; with that terrible look of settled apathy, for which the cure can be only death—or madness.

January 7th, 1870.

In the midst of a heavy thunderstorm to-day, Alan was taken ill. As I kept beside him, scattering the bush ticks which were burying themselves in his skin, I was obliged to leave our things unprotected, and so they are all spoilt. Both the dogs died this morning.

January 8th, 1870.

Alan better. One of my boys dangerously ill. I am taking quinine constantly, to ward off the fever that threateus me, but every hour I feel weaker. The scenes in the clearings are most awful. One woman—in whose tent lie three sick children—is attacking the other women almost like a wild animal. The sultry air is filled with children's sobs, and men's oaths, while some of us still work on, in quiet listlessness, or a most pathetic patience. A great malaria is rising after the heavy rain, breeding jungle fever ; yet they tell us this is the " driest and healthiest season." In the rainy season, this place is a swamp. In utter silence, we buried three children and two grown-up people this morning, and three more to-night. These silent burials leave a sadly gloomy impression on the mind, yet how can they be buried otherwise here ?

January 10th, 1870.

Quite two-thirds of us are now laid up, and the others almost useless. This oppression of damp and heat will soon become unbearable. The men are lying about more like dying dogs than human beings. How dreadfully now we feel the loss of meat. Still, nothing is to be shot, for it rains all day. Alan goes about again, though feeble and languid ; and he cheers me in his old, brave way. Sometimes I have a horrible fancy that my reason is going. I suffer unendurably from the bites of these venomous insects. It is sad to see the children (so many, but a little time ago, were plump and rosy!) wasted to mere skeletons, and to note the dogged apathy or the fierce despair of the old. I have been trying to help in one tent, where every one of the family is ill. Colonel Boyd is delirious to-night.

January 13th, 1870.

The rain has never ceased, and our tent is of little use to us now. Everything is saturated, or coated with mould. Alan's servant (who was one of the strongest and healthiest men I ever saw,) is failing fast. The whole settlement is now like a large, wet hospital, where there are neither nurses, help, nor food. We hear the voice of swearing and the voice of praying equally loud, while some of the people lie listlessly and meet the end in utter silence. God help us all!

January 14th, 1870.

Alan and I are making every effort to charter a boat. If we could only escape from this horrible grave, we might, at last, help all. Yet how hard it will be (even if we succeed) to leave these poor, helpless people behind us. I feel as if we could make a raft, if we cannot get a boat; and, though Alan looks pitifully and helplessly at my hands, I know that the very consciousness of the end for which I laboured, would give me strength. I can still—I am thankful to say—move about a little; but I am never free from mosquitoes and sand-flies.

January 17th, 1870.

Oh! this weary diary of sickness and misery! Alan's servant has just died, shrieking in delirium. Only yesterday morning he was working—harder, I think, than any of us.

So determined are we to leave if possible —knowing our lives *cannot* be spared here —that Alan and I have decided to go down the river in a small canoe which is to be had here; and try to hire, at the first negro settlement, some boat which will take us to Bolivar; as well as to obtain meat for the poor, starving people here. It will be a dangerous expedition, they tell us; but can any danger be greater than those we face here, day by day?

January 24th, 1870.

Back again in our own settlement, but, thank Heaven, only for a little time. We started at once, for is not every hour uncertain? And we reached the negro village on the evening of the day we left, the rapid current taking us down in a few hours. They made us pay £10 for a very old and unsafe boat, but I gladly pay every penny I possess to get free from this misery. We had to stay in the settlement until the 22nd, before they would consent to come back for our luggage. Our journey back, against the current, was arduous in the extreme; for we could not advance a yard, save by pulling by the bushes, all the time swarming with insects, which almost smother us, while they bite. It is impossible to describe the torture I suffer from them; even my hands are useless now. Alan says, in his quiet, grave

way, that he will make *his* serve for both.
Poor fellow, how intensely grateful he is
for the means of release, yet he dreads
leaving these emigrants to die such deaths
as we have lately witnessed.

January 25th, 1870.

We have started, and I pray that my
eyes may never again fall upon such a
heartrending scene.

"Alan," said I, most solemnly, while he
stood with his head turned away from the
wan figures on the river bank, trying to
master the sobs that shook his wasted
form; "Alan, if God gives me strength
and power in any of the future years, my
use of it shall be to bring these sufferers
release."

And Alan only whispered just one word;
his chest heaving as he looked up into the
sultry sky.

I take my last glance, through a cloud
of girlish tears, of which I am too weak to
be ashamed. The children, in a cluster,

wave their feeble little hands, but without a smile, for there is nothing of childhood left among them. The women—all with sickly, yellow faces now—bid us, for humanity's sake, hunt down the woman-fiend—who dupes and murders her victims by tens and twenties—and bring her to such poverty and misery as *they* have known. And while some of the men faintly but kindly bid us " God speed," and others turn away, either moodily envious, or un-manned by the sadness of being left behind, we repeat again our promise to intercede for them with the Governor of Bolivar. Then we pass on out of hearing, leav-ing them to their unappeased want and suffering and misery. We are taking with us one of those whom disease has left help-less, and death has left solitary.

Staying to-night at Arepau, where we got the boat, I have made a most strange and marvellous discovery—*1* of all the world ! And presently, perhaps, when we do not see so plainly the miserable

scene we left behind, or hear so drearily
the old horrible cries, we shall be able to
rejoice.   The torn fragment of an old
American newspaper had been picked up
by one of the half-castes, on the river bank,
and that paragraph was the first on which
my eyes fell—mine!—in this far-away
country, and on this isolated spot!   I try
to close my ears to the Spanish jargon of
the natives, and think over the change
which these few words may have effected
on all our future—Alan's just the same as
mine, for could I ever enjoy prosperity
now which was not shared by the dear
friend who, but for me, would have been
strong, and at ease now at *Home?*   I can
well write the paragraph from memory, so
clearly is every word fixed in my mind :—

"CHARLES MOSTYN, *grand-nephew of* ANDREW
MOSTYN, *formerly of Glasgow, Scotland, deceased.*
If the above CHARLES MOSTYN *is still alive, he is*
hereby informed that he is entitled to a LEGACY,
or INTEREST, *under the will of his great-uncle,*
ANDREW MOSTYN, *formerly of Glasgow, Scot-*

land, aforesaid, who died on the thirteenth of March, 1869, on condition that he makes claim to such legacy within twelve months from testator's decease. Applications to be made to MESSRS. COTES & FANE, *Lincoln's Inn, London, England, Solicitors for the Executors."*

" Oh, Alan !" I cry, with both my hands in his, "pray God that we may live to reach England *now!* God has put the power into my hands—*for this.* All those suffering emigrants shall be released, and shall see *home* again."

A dazed, white look creeps over Alan's face; and then, quite slowly, he falls forward, in a long and deep unconsciousness.

PART III.

FROM THE LAWYER'S NOTE-BOOK.

"The red blade broken in his hand;
And the last arrow in his quiver."

MOORE.

Lincoln's Inn,
March 12th, 1870.

COTES had just returned from Stafford, and we were talking over the case which had taken him there. He stood with his back to the fire, facing me, and I sat at the table, with my elbow on the *Gazette*, over which I had been dozing while I had awaited his arrival. The clerks had left quite an hour before, and I had locked up my desk, and was quite ready to vacate our office as soon as ever my senior had finished his narration. But when at last it did come to a close, and I had just taken out my watch as a hint, the silence of the almost empty house was suddenly broken by a rap upon our outer office—a rap that made me start strangely, although it was neither loud nor long, only so hurried and unsteady.

I opened the door, before giving myself time to conjecture who would seek us here so long after office hours, but the gas burnt too dimly in the outer office for me to distinguish who entered at my almost unwilling invitation. But as I led a stranger into the gaslight in our room, I saw Cotes look beyond me with such a surprised, fixed gaze, that I turned almost suspiciously to face this stranger as soon as I had reached my old seat, after having placed one for him. Then I felt my own gaze growing steady too—growing even painful in its questioning; so by an effort, while I felt heartily ashamed of myself, I turned my eyes from this stranger's face.

"I have no card with me, gentlemen," he said; and his voice, refined and gentlemanly, rebuked me in a moment; "but this advertisement will explain my intrusion here to-night. After to-day, my visit would be unavailing, for I am Charles Mostyn, legatee, I understand, of Mr. Andrew Mostyn, of Glasgow, under his will. Is it not so?"

We lawyers are constitutionally suspicious, and if *I* had worn eyeglasses, I should probably have put them on just then, as I saw Cotes quietly do; but yet I knew all the time that my doubt was of the flimsiest kind, and was even already rapidly melting, while I scrutinized the young man before me—for young he certainly was, though the slight figure was bowed, and the refined face was lined, as if from years of suffering, and grave, as if no smile had ever visited it, while the skin was dark and sallow, as only fever and exposure could leave a young face. And it had been so handsome once—*once!*

while I am twice his age, and feel a young man still!

"I am very glad we chanced to be here," I said, quite cordially, though the cordiality was really an effort to me, for there was growing upon me an unaccountable depression. "It was by the merest chance you found us in town. Yes, as you say, the year expires to-morrow—you recollect, Cotes?" I addressed that question to my partner solely for the purpose of forcing him to withdraw that settled gaze of his into the wan young face of our visitor, for I guessed how trying was its searching scrutiny. But it was Mr. Mostyn who answered me.

"Yes," he said, speaking low and fast, almost feverishly, "the advertisement said, unless claimed before March 13th—I remember every word."

"We had quite given up expecting any legatee—" I corrected myself, almost hurriedly, while still this strange and uncharacteristic feeling of melancholy grew upon me—"quite given up expecting you to put in any claim under the will. Indeed, Mr. Mostyn, we felt sure you must be dead, for our advertisement has gone the round of the civilized world, and we concluded that, if you *had* been living, you would have put in your claim before to-day."

"So entirely had I given up all expectation of a legatee," added Cotes, breaking his silence at last sternly, though I quite well understood the sternness to be a cloak for some other feeling, "that last week I made a calculation as to how far each nominated institution would benefit by its share of old Andrew Mostyn's wealth."

"And I doubt very much," I put in, hurriedly, because I saw a cloud fall over young Mostyn's face at these words, "whether any one of those Scotch endowments is at all in need of the old merchant's earnings."

"While I," the young man said, most quietly, "*am* in need."

"At any rate," I added, almost hastily

H 2

once more, as I turned my eyes quite away from his worn clothes and wasted figure, "the old man's grand-nephew has sole right to it."

And then, professionally, I ought either to have appointed another interview, or asked for his proofs, yet I did neither. I only awaited what he himself should say. And, stranger still, Cotes too waited, without questioning.

"Of course, at this late hour, gentlemen," young Mostyn said, still in that quiet voice, and yet as if in feverish haste, while he took out a shabby pocket-book, "I cannot detain you by any attempt to explain why your advertisement could scarcely be expected to reach me. I will only give these papers into your hands. I have had the certificates always with me, but the copies of the register I have procured only for this purpose. If you need anything more, I would refer you to—to the Reverend Herbert Wynne of Ashleigh Vicarage, Gloucestershire, whose pupil I was—living in his house for five years. And if still further——"

" Ah, yes! it will be all right," interposed Cotes, turning suddenly round with his face to the fire, and then breaking off his speech just as suddenly.

But now there had come upon me an irresistible desire to hear something of this young man's career, and so I tempted him, little by little—and even less by questioning than by silence—to tell me how it happened that he had been beyond the reach of an advertisement.

It was a sad story, though he touched it lightly—no, *lightly* is scarcely the word; he touched it shrinkingly, as if each re-collection were an open wound. But the bare outlines of fact I gathered eagerly, while my thoughts grasped a hundred that he did not touch; and I grew to under-stand a little of the tragedy to which the worn young figure and the weary face bore witness.

And all this time the refreshment we

offered—even a glass of wine alone—no persuasion could induce him to touch.

A sad story, as I said, yet a villainous one too. This young fellow has been one of the dupes of as coldly ruinous and murderous a scheme as ever entered the brain of man or woman to conceive. And this, I judge, was conceived by a woman too—a woman who, under the name, now of Mr. and now of Mrs. Matherson, has conceived (and, from her stand-point of view, successfully carried out) as devilish a fraud as ever came within my professional knowledge. Only for my intense, unaccountable interest in the young fellow who told me the story, I could not have sat to hear it out ; but when he had finished, and Cotes took up the subject—recapitulating every item, slowly, I suppose, to fix the facts on his memory—I rose and paced the room in hot impatience. But young Mostyn seemed not even to hear, as he sat with eyes fixed on the fire ; a strange, feverish light burning in them now,

totally at variance with that quiet despondency which the telling of his story
had apparently scattered.

This woman—under the name of
Matherson (so the facts fell from Cotes'
angry lips)—had sold these emigrants
land in Venezuelan Guyana which she
had no right to sell; the emigrants being
welcome to any quantity they chose to
appropriate of that dense, unhealthy,
tropical forest, reeking with pestilential
exhalations, and under water during the
wet season.

She had also—under the name of a
company—represented, by pamphlets and
letters and otherwise, that only by purchasing Land Warrants and passports
from *her* could emigrants settle in the
vacant lands of Venezuelan Guyana, or
pass their luggage through the Venezuelan
Custom House free of duty—while these
warrants were simply waste paper, and
only through the president's kindness was
the luggage passed.

She had promised to holders of two hundred pounds worth of land, a share in the stock, rights, privileges, benefits, immunities, and profits of the Company, while in reality the Company (so called!) had entirely forfeited its land by the non-fulfilment of its conditions.

"Was he correct so far?" questioned Cotes, making an abrupt stop. Then he nodded hurriedly, and with perfect comprehension, though young Mostyn had only assented by a glance, and a tightening of his lips.

"The emigrants," my partner went on, his words just a very little slower now, "many of them utterly destitute, arrived at this poisonous spot on the Caura without any of the roots, medicines, and necessaries promised them by the lady promoter. Gradually—no, we need not touch upon the time between. In the month of January last, you, having a little money left after these iniquitous purchases, succeeded in hiring an old and scarcely sea-

worthy canoe from some native settlement
lower down the river, and with a young
friend named—named——"

"The canoe, old and unsafe as it was,
would only carry five of us," put in young
Mostyn, in a low, pausing way.   "We two
friends who had gone out together—Mostyn and Fielding—the two servant lads we
had taken from Gloucestershire, and one
of the most helpless and solitary of the
settlers."

"I see, I see," interrupted Cotes, once
more, while I paused now beside the dark-
ened window. "The natives, then, who had
agreed to take you back to Ciudad Bolivar,
broke out more than once into a frenzy of
drunkenness, upon the rum they had managed to conceal in the boat.   And all this
time—all this time, while you, with one
hand, ceaselessly baled the water from the
leaking canoe, and with the other tried to
scatter the tarantulas that fell upon him
—your friend lay dying, among you and
the riotous sailors in this open boat.

Why—why, in the name of heaven, did you not take him on shore ?"

"Again and again, in his great restlessness," our visitor said, with a new heaviness in his sad voice, "he let me carry him on shore ; but presently my hand grew too unsteady, and my wrists too weak, to kill the great boa-constrictors that crept from the grass to meet us."

A little pause, and then Cotes went on, even more sternly, to all seeming.

"So, for fifteen days, you made slow way along the river, among the rocks and rapids, the alligators following in your wake. And all this time—lying exposed to the sudden rains, deafened by the quarrelsome Spanish jargon of the sailors, and blinded by the long glare of a tropical sun —your friend (in this little dangerous open boat, where you could do nothing to ease or help him, could only watch him in an agony almost as great as his own, I should say) lay hour by hour—dying."

"Dying!" repeated young Mostyn, rising

now, and standing very steadily beside the table, with his head bent upon his chest. " Until, one morning—in the sunrise—I saw just a little extra shadow creep into the eyes that used to—that—that—I mean that for so long had been dim and powerless to meet mine. And—I *knew*. Oh, God! how close I held him then, while the boys fought those poisonous insects, for life indeed, and—*death!*"

" You landed at Bolivar, and then——"

" Then," said the young man, answering Cotes' question in a different tone—the hurried, quiet, feverish tone with which he had begun his recital—" every kindness was offered me, and we laid him in a quiet spot, which I can easily find again when I—go back."

"Go back!" I echoed, simply because I could not help the words leaving my lips, as I watched him.

"Yes, could I stay here?" he asked, drawing one thin hand wearily across his forehead, "while I know what other men

are suffering out there; while I can picture
the labour and the famishing of women and
children; while I can remember the haggard faces we left behind? Why, I see
them night and day—with always among
them, clearest of all, that one worn, shadow-
ed face that used to be so different.
Could I bear to stay here and be one
amongst such people as I have met in your
streets to-day—surrounded by wealth and
ease and luxury; while all the time I
know what could be done, and who could
be rescued, by this wealth, which—"

"You are right," said Cotes, a little irrelevantly, but with unwonted gentleness, as
the young fellow paused, with indrawn lips
and heaving chest; "but it is all too difficult a problem for you to solve, at your
years. Why, even we lawyers cannot do
it. Do you intend to go back at once then,
to this infernal spot, and waste all old
Andrew Mostyn's money at a blow?"

"As soon as I feel that it is mine," was
the quiet answer, "I shall go. Then—after

that—I have a—a debt to settle, before I rest."

He paused only one minute, then raised his head as he went on, nervously closing and unclosing his thin fingers; "I must find the woman who duped and deceived us. I must see her suffer agony equal to *this*. I must hear her cry in vain for help—as we left them crying on the river shore that day. I must know her pray that the long days and heavy nights may be cut short—as we have prayed. I must know her life barren of the trust and faith she robbed us of. I must see the health and vigour pass from her frame in single drops of agony—as it passed from those whose strength she stole, and whose vigorous life she took more cruelly than murderer ever did his work before. Then, when this money has done its work, I——I——"

"You will come in and thank *us*," I put in, with, I am afraid, a rather futile attempt at animation, "for being the irresponsible means of placing this power in your hands.

And, for myself, I know I shall be heartily glad to see you, Mr. Mostyn."

For hours after we had all parted, indeed for that whole night, I could not free my thoughts from that story of young Mostyn's. It was not as if I had simply read the account of that fraudulent scheme. But I had witnessed, all the while I heard of it, the cruel ravages it had made on a young fellow who, I could see, had once been strong and spirited and fearless. I had seen the traces of want and fever in his eyes, and felt how much must have been borne before an unsuspicious and manly nature could give birth to such a fiery hatred as he bears to that woman, who planned their ruin, and who is, possibly, duping others every day. For young Mostyn had heard that another ship load of ruined creatures are on their way to that miserable doom. Then, sixty he left behind him (only thirty remaining of his own party), and he is sure that their supply of beans and rice was but barely sufficient for

a week. And they had nothing besides, save
the medicines which had been kindly supplied to them by the governor of Bolivar—
Heaven help them!

This will make Cotes sneer more than
ever over the credulity of our nineteenth
century. Well, I can only hope that that
unscrupulous woman's craft will not save
her, and—I will think of it no more, it only
serves to depress a man.

March 18th, 1870.

Old Andrew Mostyn's legacy is paid over
to his grand-nephew. The papers were all
so straightforward, we had scarcely anything
to do. He has just been in to thank us, and
bid us good-bye, as he leaves England to-day.
His week's rest here in town has changed
him very little, and it strikes me he can
never regain the strength and elasticity of
young manhood, even if he ever loses that
feverish unrest. I hardly understand what
he has gone to do, for there is something
about him which checks all personal ques-

tioning—something I cannot define even to myself.

Another thing I could not quite understand. He would never accept the slightest and smallest act of hospitality from either of us.

November 11*th*, 1870.

One of the densest fogs even I can remember. Cotes had not been into town at all, and I was just wishing I had followed his example, when a card was brought in to me, from a gentleman who requested a private interview. I took the card up to the gas and tried to read it, but I had been staring out into the yellow fog, and could not distinguish the faint letters on the card.

"A stranger, sir," the clerk put in, as if to assist me; "quite a stranger to us."

I gave him a sign that the stranger might come, and waited, still holding the card in my hand.

Just as if the fog had bewildered him, as

it had bewildered me, he came into my office with one hand shading his eyes; and when he dropped it I started a little, not because I had recognised the young man who had come so unexpectedly eight months ago to claim that legacy under old Andrew Mostyn's will, but because, while I recognised him so easily, there was *something* I could *not* recognise in the straight, fixed gaze and the spiritless, low voice.

"Can you spare me half an hour?" he asked, taking no notice of my outstretched hand. "I would like to tell you the end of the story to which you once listened so patiently. Then——"

"I shall be delighted," I said; but, try as I would, I found it impossible to feel delighted. I went round and made him take a seat at the table, just for the rest it would be to myself to escape, for a moment, the curious questioning of the wistful, perplexed gaze; and when he had taken this seat, and leaning forward on the table

lowered his eyes at last, I went back to
my seat opposite.

"Do you remember what I told you of
—my friend?" he asked, speaking very
slowly, and as if he found it difficult to
choose or form his words.

"Every word," I answered, as cheerily
as I could; while he took out a pocket-
book and slowly turned over the letters
and papers it contained, until he drew a
photograph from among them, and in the
same slow, gentle way gave it into my
hand.

It was the photograph of a tall, white
cross, standing amid beautiful tropical
trees and flowers; but just as unable was
I to read the words upon it as I had been
to read Mr. Mostyn's card.

"You remember," he questioned, after
having waited in vain for me to read the
name upon the grave, "how my friend
died upon the Orinoco? That is his grave.
He lies in the Protestant corner of the
beautiful cemetery near Bolivar, and there

creeps across his grave that cool, whispering shadow of the palms, which he used to
say would flit across our own homes in
that beautiful new country to which—he
thought we were going. His name is
there upon the cross; will you try to read
it? And there is one of the verses that he
loved. He sang it—feebly, O so feebly
I could scarcely hear him—on that last
terrible day upon the river.

> ' Nothing in my hand I bring,
> Simply to—Thy cross I cling.'

He was robbed of all that he *could* bring;
health and manhood, love and trust;
he was robbed of all, and yet he said
he could go—with nothing—in his hand.
His Saviour knew, he said. And often and
often he used to say our Saviour walked
beside us—in that awful voyage—when
for fifteen days he lay there—dying. O
God, how terrible it was to take that
voyage again, and how there came back to
me ceaselessly his brave and feeble words

of hope, and each patient, trustful
prayer !"

"It was not wise of you to take that
voyage again," I said, looking vaguely
down upon the photograph, while a terrible surmise began to creep slowly into my
mind. "You chose a beautiful spot for
your friend's grave though, Mr. Mostyn;
and I am very much obliged to you for
showing me this."

"I wished you to see," he said, in slow,
short sentences, "that his grave is just
what he might have chosen; and that
it will be honoured and cared for there;
and to hear exactly what I have done with
the money which—you said—Charles Mostyn legally inherited. And I hope you
will feel that his money—was used—
kindly—and pitifully."

I was on the point of interposing that I
already felt quite sure of this, when again
he raised his eyes to my face; and again
their strange, fixed, and yet questioning
look silenced me.

"That forest land," he said, "no longer buries youth and health and manhood; no longer withers hope and trust and courage. Those whom we left behind us there a year ago, have homes now in other lands, where they can work and hope. Life is no longer a ghastly living death to them, They were nourished and tended on the homeward journey, and they no longer walk wearily through the day, and moan the night away. They had means given them to begin a fresh career in healthy homes, and I have seen them all—happy. So changed—so changed !"

A little pause followed the slow words, but I could not break it.

"And this," he went on presently, his breath quickening, "has been done with the money you had in trust for——"

"But the money alone could not have accomplished this," I put in, wondering over his sudden pause. "The good could not have been done by old Mostyn's money

without the care and time and generosity
of old Mostyn's nephew."

"It was *I* who went back," he answered,
with a strange breathlessness and hurry
in his low, pausing tones. "It was *I* who
brought them away from that great yawn-
ing grave. And when I took that voyage
again, and I remembered Charlie's gentleness and patience, I said I would leave—
that *other* task undone. I would leave all
punishment to—my God. So I try to
forget who did us—this wrong. I went .
with the emigrants, and afterwards made
it all easy for them. I saw them again,
hopeful and happy. I prayed God bless
them in their new homes, and—and I
came on to tell you—all."

The strange and terrible suspicion
of dementia, which must have had birth
almost from the moment the young man
had come in to me this morning, had
grown now so painful and so powerful
that I felt my heart beating as if I had
been a girl instead of a middle-aged

lawyer ; while now I read so much more in that dazed, wide glance of his, and in the broken, hurried words.

"You speak of your friend as *Charlie*," I said, in a forced, measured way that sounded unfamiliar to me.   "It is strange that your baptismal names should have been the same."

"I remember," he went on, throwing back his head, and clasping both hands upon his forehead, "that, as we stood in the boat on that day we left the settlement, he and I—Charlie and I—he said—hundreds of times the words had to haunt me, in his own earnest voice, before I *could* come to you and claim—*his* money.   He said—with both his hands in mine, and a look upon his face as if the words were prayer—'Alan, God has put the power into my hands *for this*. All these suffering emigrants shall be released, and shall see *Home* again.'"

"*His* money !" I echoed, for though there had so surely dawned on me the

suspicion, indeed, I may say the convic-
tion, of latent insanity, I had still had no
conception of fraud."

" *His* money. Charlie's money," my client
answered, while there came a faint, wistful
smile to his lips that was pitiful to see—
"Charlie's money. I remember how he
took both my hands in his while the vow
passed his lips. His money should be
used to rescue those poor creatures, and
bring them Home. It *has* rescued them.
It *has* brought them Home."

"And you?" I asked, for I had not the
faintest notion what to say.

" I—have finished my work now. There
is a little of Charlie's money to give back
to you, and then——"

He broke off there, unclasping his hands
and drawing them slowly across each
temple.

"I have sometimes fancied that my
brain would grow useless—too soon. But
it has lasted, and now it will be well for

me to be—they will understand at our old home—under—medical care."

The strange, quiet words unmanned me as I believe I never was unmanned before, and I bent my head upon my hands, and shut out that pitiful, bewildered gaze.

"I am not afraid," he said, speaking in a wistful, gentle whisper, yet so clearly that I could not miss one word. "I have done all there was for me to do, and—presently, perhaps they will tell me I—am better. I always was stronger than Charlie. I am not afraid. I knew it must come. I knew it must come—soon. I only feared it might be before—you knew. As I came here to-day, I thought at first that what they called—the fog—was only about *me;* clinging to me only; and I hurried—with it—glad that it hid my face from—other men, but terrified that it should close me in—too soon—before I had told you that—Charlie died, and I—was spared. Now I do not mind.

I know it will be well for me—now—to be
watched. The law has punishment in
store for me, I know, but it can come
afterwards; when I—am stronger. Are
you so pitiful—*you*—that you cannot look
up? Ah! if you had known—what it was
—*before*—when I watched him die. Or
afterwards, when every hour of every day
—and night—was haunted by the misery
—of others! Now—at last it is over.
Charlie himself has turned this misery
to joy—as he said he would—and you
need not pity me—*now*. I am not afraid."

REAPING THE WHIRLWIND.

REAPING THE WHIRLWIND.

CHAPTER I.

THE breakfast-table was drawn quite into the window-recess, though a fire blazed in the low grate; and the window was thrown wide open, though over the bare uplands behind this pretty little lodging-house the chill November shadows crept. For it was very softly and tenderly that the wind sailed inland from that grey line of Autumn sea; and they were very gentle kisses that it left upon the two young thoughtful faces lifted with such readiness to meet it.

"Who would imagine this a November morning?" Joyce Heringham said. Her hat lay on a chair beside her, her hands were locked upon the table, and her delicate face was tinted daintily by that early walk of hers beside the sea. "Why should we go abroad in search of Summer, Eve, when Summer is here in Ventnor?"

Evelyn Carmichael sat nominally presiding over the little dual breakfast, but her eyes were wandering far over the sea, and her hands lay idly on an open letter. For a few moments Joyce watched her face with a half-smile; then, happening to catch sight of an empty envelope, Miss Heringham's eyes opened widely and wonderingly.

"Why, Evelyn, have you really and truly received a letter at last? My dear, this is the only one you've had since I knew you first, nearly—how many years ago?"

"Just nine years," Evelyn answered quietly.

"Yes, nine years; and yet I never saw you receive a letter before, Eve. Now," she added, with a swift change of tone, as she saw how her companion's face had paled, "suppose we begin breakfast. You would have had more appetite, dear, if you had been with me in my walk."

Yet even as Joyce spoke, her own delicate colour faded, and her knife and fork were left untouched.

"I want to tell you about this letter," Evelyn said, speaking slowly, as she filled the coffee-cups, "and—it is *not* the only one I have received since you and I first met nine years ago. It is the second; and, like the last, it has followed me from place to place, until its writer must imagine that it is lost—I hope he does."

"Then," said Joyce calmly, though she wondered over the last few hurried words, "you never answered that one. Are they love-letters, Eve?"

The girl's lips broke into a smile, but it was so sad and dreamy that her friend would rather have seen them ever so grave.

"What should I do if they were?" Joyce went on, turning her attention suddenly to her plate. "How could I spare you? Happy as we two girls are together, we are so thoroughly alone in the world, Eve, that, if one of us found other ties and other interests, I—I cannot fancy solitude more intense, or loneliness more utter, for the one who would be left."

"If we ever separate, Joyce," said Evelyn, with the old natural smile which her friend felt it so good to see again, "it will be by *your* wish, or *your* act, never by mine. For nine years you have been my—my——"

"'My own, my guiding star,'" hummed Joyce, intent upon her breakfast.

"My good angel in every way," said Evelyn, carrying one of the cups to her friend's seat, simply as an excuse to stoop and kiss her. "Think what a desolate, unloved child I was on that first night at school, when you, the favourite there, took me at once to be your little friend. Think of how you helped and cared for me through the five years we spent together there, and of how different that time would have been for me without your love and guidance. Think of the day you left; when in my misery I dared not say good-bye, but stood far off, defying the grief which was breaking my heart, and which kept me so long afterwards in that solitary sick-room of mine. Think of the day when you met me on the threshold of your own home, because, finding my life unbearable without you, I had left school alone in the darkness, and found my way on foot to you—famished, perished, and footsore. Think of how tenderly you took me in, and led me to your mother's side, and kissed me there, and asked her to let us be sisters; and how from that very day —through everything—you have been a sister indeed. No; don't interrupt me, Joyce. I remember all these things even if you—because they have been only a few among the great and generous actions of your life—forget them. And now think whether I could of my own will ever leave the home you gave me, and the one dear friend who is the whole world to me."

"I am very thankful to hear that," said Joyce Heringham, speaking as easily as she could, and looking away from her companion's flushing cheeks and wistful eyes. "I am not afraid of anything now, and you may have as many letters as you like, Eve—even sealed and blue and formidable epistles like this first specimen."

"This is a lawyer's letter," said Evelyn Carmichael, her hand upon the paper while she spoke; "and so was that first letter I received a year ago. And, as I left that one unanswered, Joyce, ·I shall leave this one unanswered too."

There was a few moments' silence then, while Joyce wondered whether it would be more kind to question her friend, or to pass by this low and broken half-confidence. Then the warm, sympathetic nature of the girl dictated, as usual, the kinder way, and she asked her next question in that tone of earnestness which makes a response so easy.

"Is it a business letter only, Eve, or do you personally know the gentleman who writes to you?"

"Only a business letter," Evelyn answered, "yet I *have* known personally the gentleman who sends it. Mr. Pratman used, even long ago, to be the friend of——"

In the unexpected pause, Joyce asked her question coolly—

"Mr. Pratman is a lawyer then, and it is he who wrote you the two letters?"

"Yes," said Evelyn, speaking absently. "He used to come very often to Hilton Guise, not on business with my step-father only; for—I said it before, didn't I?—he was the great friend of Horace Rohan."

A strange, disappointed shadow fell over Joyce Heringham's listening face. For fourteen years she had been Evelyn Carmichael's nearest and dearest, indeed, 'to all appearance, *only* friend, yet never before had she heard these two names which Eve uttered now so thoughtfully. Still there was no taint of suspicion in her heart, and it was only in real sympathy that she questioned once more.

"Do you remember this Mr. Pratman?"

"Yes, I should know him—I think; though of course he could not know me, as I was a child when I used to see him at Hilton Guise. I was only ten when—when I left it for ever."

"Eve," said Joyce, laying one hand gently on her friend's, as she looked into her anxious face, "tell me of that time. I have never asked you before, all through these nine years, and I would not ask you now in idle curiosity. But, if *I* had had a trouble, dear, however long ago, I should tell it all to you, and feel better for doing so."

There was a little pause, but Joyce was not discouraged by this. She seemed to feel the difficulty for Evelyn as if it had been her own, and helped her then, as she had helped her ever.

"Eve, your mother married a Mr. Rohan, of Hilton Guise, did she not? I remember long ago (when we were girls at school, and I used to tell you so much of my mother and my home, while you told me nothing) that I grew to feel quite certain that your mother's could not have been a happy marriage for her."

"*For her?*" echoed Evelyn, locking her fingers tightly in her lap, while her breath came quickly and irregularly. "For my mother? Oh! Joyce, she *might* have been so very, very happy!"

"Then," asked Joyce, understanding now (as she saw her old fancy broken into atoms) why she had never heard a word of blame of her step-father uttered by Evelyn, "your step-father was not unkind to you?"

"Never," Evelyn answered, in a tearless sob. "He was always good and kind to

me. It was—oh! Joyce, dear friend, do
not make me say hard words of my own
mother!"

"No, dear. And Mr. Rohan, your
mother's husband, had a son, had he?"

"Yes, one son, an only child. Oh! to
think, Joyce, of my mother separating
them—father and son!"

"Perhaps——" began Joyce, gently.

But Eve stopped her, speaking low, and
with a great sadness in her far-off gaze.

"I know what you would say, Joyce, but
it was not so. Mr. Rohan took us—his
wife and her little girl—from our small
house and narrow life to his beautiful
home. Oh! Joyce, think what it was to
me to live my child-life at Hilton Guise,
with such a father at its head, and with
such a—such a brother!"

"And were you not happy?"

"Ah, so happy—so very, very happy—
for a time, though I seemed to know how
each day the happiness grew less, as she
slowly set his father's heart against him!"

"But why? Could she have been jealous of her husband's love for his own son?"

"Yes," said Evelyn, with a shudder, "jealous of his place in his father's heart, and—jealous of his right to his father's home and wealth; jealous in many ways," she repeated, drearily, " of him who, while he was so good to her little girl, was so— so unsuspicious of her. At last—I say at last, and yet it came so quickly—the secret work was finished, and the open rupture came. Oh! Joyce, often even now that hour comes back to me in my troubled dreams, though so many years lie over its grave."

"They quarrelled, you mean?" asked Joyce, gently laying her hand upon her friend's bent head.

"They quarrelled," Evelyn answered, in a sobbing whisper; " the father and son; while my mother, who had caused it, stood and listened. Oh! Joyce, if through all his years of exile Horace Rohan has hated every woman, I—I could never blame him."

"But, Eve," pleaded Joyce, "are you so sure that she *only* was to blame?"

"So sure," faltered Evelyn, with a pain in every uttered word, "that you will be merciful to me, Joyce, and ask me no more."

"I must ask you more, dear," Joyce persisted, in real kindness, while she interrupted her own words with a gentle kiss; "much more. And you will tell me; not only to-day, but on other days too, as we two live our quiet life together; for never again, my dear, never again, shall any painful secret be kept between us. Did Horace Rohan leave his home in consequence of what—Mrs. Rohan said?"

"Yes. He could do nothing else, after his father's wrath had so skilfully been turned against him. Yes, he went, and—there was no one then to stand between her and her ambition."

"Hush, dear! Had they—the father

and son—been loving and united before this?"

"Before my mother's marriage," spoke Evelyn, very low, "they were—as I have often and often heard, and as I could see, even I, so young a child—most united. And they were both brave and true and generous. Everyone loved them."

"The son was grown up, Eve; a companion to his father?"

"Yes, he was one-and-twenty, I think, when I, a child of nine, saw him first."

"What was he like?" asked her friend, speaking almost cheerfully now, as she feigned to be busily cutting bread.

"I—forget."

"Then," pursued Joyce, determined not to be silenced just yet, nor to let the cloud of secrecy and solitude fall again on Evelyn's thoughts, "you would not know him now?"

"I—think so; but he could not know me."

"I suppose not; your face seems even

to me quite different from what it was fourteen years ago," said Joyce, with a smile.

"Yet, do you know," observed Evelyn, with a faint reflection of the smile, "only yesterday I was mistaken for you—*you*, of whom we were so proud at school, you know, while I was such a sickly, puny child."

"I almost wonder," mused Joyce, passing this speech by, as her thoughts fled back to that arrival at the seaside school of the shy, trembling child to whom her heart had gone out so pitifully, and in whom she had never since that day felt a moment's disappointment, "how it was that your mother could spare her only child from that great beautiful home she had won."

"I fretted. I fretted myself ill," said Evelyn, below her breath, "and she was *obliged* to send me away."

"And you never went home afterwards?"

"Never. I have never been home since
—oh, Joyce, how could I go?"

"I see," said Joyce, almost cheerfully.
"I know all about your leaving, dear, and
how you came to me—as, of course, it was
wise and kind of you to do. And we've
been together ever since, haven't we? So
now tell me of your two solitary letters.
They were both, you say, from the gentleman who is legal adviser to Mr. Rohan of
Hilton Guise? I suppose that first letter
told you of your mother's death, a year
ago?"

"At that time," returned Evelyn, avoid-
ing her friend's gaze, "Mr. Pratman wrote
me a letter of advice; a very kind letter it
was, and wise, perhaps, but he gave no
advice which I could follow. He said that
as Mr. Rohan was alone at Hilton Guise it
would be wise of me to return to him, and
take his absent son's place. *Take his son's
place!*" reiterated the girl, with intense
bitterness. "The son whom we had
driven from his home!"

"*We?*"

"Yes, we; the strangers to whom
Horace had been so kind. Could I separate myself from my mother? When we
had driven him away, could I arrogate
his place in his father's home and affec-
tion?"

"Then you took no notice of this
advice?"

"I took no notice; but—but Mr. Pratman said more than that, Joyce, and I
should like to tell you all now. He said
that Mr. Rohan wished for my return at
once, as he was about to make his will and
leave me his—his sole heiress; that I had
always been a favourite of his, and I
should have no care or responsibility for
my future, from the day I returned to him.
He told me also—it almost seemed as if he
had suspected how I should receive this
offer—that a reconciliation between Horace
and his father was utterly impossible; that
Horace had no chance of being reinstated
in his father's affections, or mentioned in

his father's will, and so it would do no harm to *him* if I took his place, and that it would be discreet and politic in me to do so."

"I suppose," put in Joyce, as Evelyn almost breathlessly ceased speaking, "Mr. Pratman must have fancied that you never received that letter ?"

"I suppose so. I never heard again until this morning."

"And now ?"

"Now he writes to tell me that my— that Mr. Rohan of Hilton Guise is dead, and urges me to return for the funeral ; as I" —the low, troubled voice sank to a very whisper here—"as I inherit Hilton Guise, and the whole of his property."

"My dear," cried Joyce, involuntarily starting to her feet, "can this be true ?"

"Will you read the letter?"

"Not yet. I would rather hear it all from you. Do you really mean to say that Mr. Rohan has left you his property ? Oh, Evelyn, what a shame—I mean—for-

give me, but it seems *so* strange and unnatural—just yet."

Evelyn Carmichael's reception of this
spontaneous opinion, was as unexpected as
was the information which had evoked it;
and Joyce's eyes filled with tears as Evelyn
slipped to the ground, uttering eager,
broken words of thanks.

" I thought," she faltered, her eyes very
wide and earnest, in spite of the gathering
tears; "I *feared* you would not see the
wrong; I *feared* that you would bid me
go."

" But perhaps you may be forced to go ?"
questioned Joyce, gently.

" *Go!*" cried the girl, with flashing eyes
and quivering lips.   " Go to be mistress of
the house from which Horace was driven ?
Go to claim the property which was stolen
from Horace ?   Go to usurp the fealty of
his own people who had loved him ? I,
who know how he was slandered ? *I* live
in his old home, wanting nothing—while
he——"

"Eve, dear Eve," whispered Joyce,
soothingly, though in real alarm, as Evelyn
stopped, her whole frame shaken by her
sobs, "I see it just as you see it, and we
two are not going to separate. Hush, my
dear! Let us just talk sensibly for a few
minutes, and you will see that it will all
end rightly, and fit itself at last into the
wonderful puzzle, as every atom in the
great creation does, if we only wait and
see.—Ah, a little smile at last, dear!
That's right. I have hardly known our
room this morning, because I missed your
smile so much. Grave as this pale face
of yours can be, its smile belongs to it so
thoroughly that I can scarcely recognise
it without. Now is the coffee cold, or
shall we finish breakfast? Take your old
seat, dear, and you shall listen while I
draw a lively picture of the return of the
prodigal son—I mean," she corrected,
literally frightened by Evelyn's deepening
pallor, "of the happy return of Horace
Rohan to the home of his forefathers, and

our happier departure for warmer lands, where we are to find our long lost roses, and grow out of these narrow dresses of ours. Oh, dear, dear, I wish we could presently emerge, Eve, into a pair of stalwart young women, with broad hands and waists, and a settled cherry-colour in our cheeks! When we come back from Italy, in that thriving and altogether pleasant condition, we will go over to Hilton Guise some day, and hover about the place in disguise, like sensation-novel detectives, to see the Squire of Hilton enjoy his own again. Stay a moment, while I ring for warm eggs and coffee; then give me your opinion of this project."

"In this letter," said Evelyn, laying her open letter beside Joyce's plate, "Mr. Pratman tells me that, however I act in this matter—again he seems to have a suspicion of my unwillingness to take Mr. Rohan's property, you see, Joyce—I can in no way benefit Horace. No possible act of mine can restore his birthright to him.

No living man or woman, he says," Evelyn went on, the words slowly passing her pale lips, " can change his fortune now. Hilton Guise is mine, and through my whole life I have no power to part with it."

" That means," put in Joyce, musingly, as she returned to her place, " that only by your *will* could it revert to its legal owner."

" Yes," echoed Evelyn, drearily, " it means that never through all my life can I see justice done to one whom my mother injured; only by my death can he be restored to his lawful position."

" Then," said Joyce, again speaking easily only by a great effort, "the decision seems taken out of your own hands, Eve. Whether you wish it or not, you *must* be the mistress of Hilton Guise."

" Joyce," returned her friend, with a sudden change of tone and expression, " of course, if you have dismissed me, I must find another dwelling somewhere—I don't say another home, for no spot on earth can ever be home to me while you are living elsewhere—but, if you have not dismissed me (and I pray and believe you can never be so cruel) let us leave England to-morrow instead of next week, but leave it together as we always meant to do."

" How can we, dear ? Even if it is possible for you to come, you will have so much to arrange first with Mr. Pratman."

"I have nothing to arrange with him," said Evelyn, steadily. " He will never know that I have read his letter."

" It must have been many days on the road," observed Joyce, reading the different postmarks on the envelope.

"It shall travel no farther though," returned Evelyn, with a faint, swift smile, as she crossed the room, and laid the sheet on the fire. " There, now I feel free once more, Joyce ; and—may we start for Italy to-morrow ?"

" To-day, dear, if you like," said Joyce

Heringham, in her prompt, generous way. "That would be safer, perhaps, for fear this friend of yours should determine to execute a personal search for you. There is nothing to keep us here, and we have scarcely unpacked at all, so we shall have no trouble. But—but I'm afraid you will not escape all you wish to escape, even by your absence from England, dear. You will be advertised for, and—Eve, I'm afraid you have not thought this over quite properly yet. Do you forget that now Hilton Guise must be unoccupied, the land and tenants neglected, the income accumulating, and no good done to anyone?—In such information as this, my dear, you reap the benefit of my being a barrister's daughter —and do you feel sure that you are acting wisely? May you not be utterly mistaken, in this generous, humble impulse of yours?"

"I do not know," whispered Evelyn wearily. "I only know I can never take a farthing of that property which ought to have been Horace's; and I could not live one hour taking his place in the home which is really his."

Silence followed the girl's steady, tired words; and she sat again in utter stillness, looking far through the open window, to the gray line of sea.

"I think," said Joyce, simply for the sake of breaking this silence, "Mr. Pratman—if he is a clever man of the law—would laugh a good deal could he hear this very unbusinesslike discussion of ours, Eve. I often think what an ignorant and unstable pair we are, to be wandering about the world at will, and—and," she added, full sadly, "with so little strength between us too. Did you hear those people on the deck of the steamer yesterday, whispering of us, and saying they didn't know which looked the frailer of the two?"

There was no answer beyond the faintest smile; and Joyce made her next remark in a tone which was cheerful only by a great effort.

"Eve, do you know it is possible we may meet Horace Rohan abroad—*Mr. Rohan*, I ought to say, only you see I have just been thinking of him as your brother. It is quite possible, dear."

"I dare not meet him," said Evelyn, while the red rose hotly and slowly to her brow, as Joyce had never seen it rise before. "I dare not hear the words he might so justly and so truthfully say to me."

"Now another cup of coffee, please, Eve. I'm rather in a hurry to begin my packing."

"Joyce, Joyce, how good you are to me! But, oh, look away, dear friend. I am not like myself to-day, and cannot meet your loving, tender gaze."

CHAPTER II.

EVEN lying as it did in the very heart of town; and surrounded by the roar and rumble of London traffic, one corner of Lincoln's Inn Fields had had a pitying touch of shadow on it through all that heavy and oppressive June day; and now that the sun had rested from its fierce glare down upon the streets, and had grown lovely above the western lands, one corner house even here looked calm and cool in the silence. And eyes that had grown very tired of looking on legions of closed and dusty window-panes, glanced with a sigh of real refreshment to those two narrow upper windows, thrown wide open to a miniature forest of Summer flowers.

Toiling slowly up the steep and angular staircase of this house, a woman went, with a child in her arms—a heavy, white-faced child, with overhanging brow and undersized limbs.

"Mother," she whispered, dropping her head on the woman's shoulder, "take me in to see the flowers again."

"Presently," the mother answered, in a hurried whisper; standing aside upon a corner stair and waiting, as a door closed above and a slow and steady step began to descend the stairs.

"Now," persisted the sick child, querulously, comprehending no motive for the suppression of her longings. "You promised I should see the flowers when the gentleman went out. Mother, take me now."

"Hush, dear!" urged the woman nervously, for the gentleman they spoke of had reached them now, in his slow descent of the upper staircase; and he might hear the sick child's entreaty, and be angry to find that she was speaking of his own private room. But, if he were, he certainly showed it unusually, for he stopped and spoke to the mother, while he lightly touched the wan baby face.

"Is she better to-day?"

"It's so hot, sir," explained the mother, anxiously evading the negative. "The heat makes her languid, and a little peevish."

"There's a pleasant little breeze blowing into my room," the gentleman said, "and it makes the flowers lift their heads. Perhaps it may make the little one do so too; take her in and try. Here is the key. You will have an hour undisturbed while I am away, and I know how quietly you two can sit there, looking out over the Fields—sounds pleasant, doesn't it? though it raises notions that are all false, of cowslips, and of waving shadows on the corn."

"Some day, sir," returned the woman, detecting no tone of irony in the clear, kind voice, "I tell her, she'll be as fond of these Fields as of the greenest in the world—when she's lived here as long as I have."

"I hope she may," he said, more sadly than incredulously; and somehow the woman's eyes filled with tears as, with a curtsey, she took the offered key.

Quite an hour's rest she had won for herself in the quiet, pleasant room, and of fresh air, flower-scented, for her tired child; when the gentleman returned to it.

"That's well," he said, when he saw the little girl lying placidly asleep in her mother's arms, with a faint flush in her cheeks. "Stay, I have brought her a few strawberries. They will do her no harm, and if I put a flower on the basket, she will think it all the prettier when she awakes. Nonsense! There is no need of thanks."

As the woman closed the door gently behind her, this solitary lodger of hers stood before the open window, just where she had been sitting, and looked out over a forest of roofs to the line of sky beyond. And while he did so, the compassion which had been upon his face died slowly from it, and a look of inflexible severity wholly took its place. It was not an old face either, nor a hardened one, though that one furrow on the low, stern brow should not have deepened thus while only half the allotted years of a man's life had been told. But it was the face of a man who had lived *much*, and who moved onward with no willing step, and looked backward with no yearning memory.

He turned from the window presently, suddenly and swiftly, as if forcing himself to snap the long and painful thought which enchained him; and just as he did so there was a long, quick rap upon his door. Scarcely waiting for the invitation to enter —perhaps because it was not very readily accorded—a tall, showily-dressed girl advanced into the room, and smiled graciously upon its occupant.

"Miss Vermont," he said, with a quite perceptible chilliness in his tones, "this is an unexpected—intrusion."

"You are frank, as usual, Mr. Rohan," the girl said, with a laugh, as she ensconced herself in a seat opposite to him, and made a surreptitious effort to draw forward a few folds into her tightly-fitting dress of tawdry silk; "but I knew what to expect before I came, and so I shall speak out all the same."

"I am very sorry to hear it."

"I know many a young lady," she said, looking with a straight, free look into his eyes, "who would be utterly quenched by such a remark as that from *you*, and would leave you at once. But I am not—as I have told you before—easily depressed."

"Again I can only say I am very sorry to hear it."

Horace Rohan said this very calmly, as he sat leaning with one arm on the table, the very picture of indolence and indifference only—to those who could not read

the fiercer, stronger passions so easily
stirred within this cynical and solitary
nature.

His visitor to-day could not read them,
even in that steady gaze of hers; and so
she answered the words of quiet scorn
with another laugh, while she minutely investigated every item in the room; the
flowers, the open piano, the well-filled
bookshelves, the piles of music on the table,
the pictures on the walls—so few but so
beautiful—the terrier on the hearth, and,
last and longest of all, the owner of these
things, who, she complacently ruminated,
must of necessity listen now, undisturbed,
to an old and oft-denied request, because
she had successfully at last invaded this
privacy of his.

"Mr. Rohan," she began, smiling co-
quettishly, as she gingerly touched her
plaits, as if to satisfy herself that they
were where she expected them to be, and
then smoothed down the thick, straight
locks upon her forehead, " don't I deserve

just one little compliment for my clever-
ness in tracing you from your publisher's?
I knew I should succeed some day, though
they would not give me your address.
When I met you last at the Music Hall,
and told you this, you thought I should
fail, didn't you?"

"I hoped you would," observed Horace,
icily. "But, as you did not, tell me the
object of your visit."

"Oh, you know it! You know I want
permission to sing your songs on my pro-
vincial tour. You know how indefatigably
I have sought this permission from you;
and now I intend to coax it out of you."

"I could not imagine *that* to be the
motive of your visit to-day," said Horace
Rohan, rising as he spoke, "because I have
before answered you the question, decisively
and finally. I have no power to grant that
reiterated request of yours, Miss Vermont.
I write only for one man, as you know; and
he buys from me every right in every song I
compose—as you also know."

"But I feel sure," persisted the girl, tapping the carpet complacently with one of her high-heeled shoes, "that he would be willing to concede *to you* in this one case, if you would make it a personal request of your own. He would grant anything to you. Come, Mr. Rohan, I am sure you are going to consent. A gentleman never refuses the request of a lady, you know."

"But perhaps you have misnamed—us both."

"That's why I came myself," concluded the girl, without pausing to define his meaning. "Now, Mr. Rohan, please consent at once. Your songs suit me exactly."

"Then their mission," said Horace, in a pausing, ironical tone, "is fulfilled."

"And I will make them," she pursued, her eyes following him as he went up to the chimney-piece and stood leaning against it, "still more popular even than they are. There! I'm sure that pleasant prospect is irresistible to a composer. You have only need to testify that I am a promising and rising artiste, and that you yourself have taken an interest in me."

"But I have not," observed Horace, slowly and unmistakably.

" Oh, how cruel you are trying to be," she said, with a pouting pretence of mis-understanding him, "just to save yourself one little minute of trouble ! We all know you are a gentleman, Mr. Rohan, in spite of your living so quietly here, and selling your compositions. Now tell me honestly, could you, as a gentleman, persist in refus-ing so trifling a request from a lady ?"

"No lady would have obliged me to do this again and again—as I have had to do."

"What an unkind remark," cried Miss Vermont, raising her hands deprecatingly, "after I had asserted so willingly that we all acknowledge you to be a gentleman !"

"Pray don't waste your valuable time discussing me," requested Horace, sternly. "Let me tell you once for all that, honour-ably, I could not accede to your persistent request; and therefore I shall not do it."

"You are so strange, Mr. Rohan," said the girl, with feigned simplicity. "Most men are easily influenced by women."

"No woman," observed Horace, with a stern compression of his lips, "could ever influence me."

"I do believe," she said, with an inquisitive gaze into the handsome, cynical face, "that you must have had some disappointment in your life, caused by a woman."

"I have indeed. This visit is a great disappointment to me, and—caused by a woman."

There was little room in Miss Vermont's cheeks for nature's signals to assert themselves, but she was conscious just then of an uncomfortable sensation, as if it would have relieved her to blush, if such a thing had been possible.

"Don't imagine you have done with me," she remarked, flippantly, as she prepared to leave. "You will relent, I'm sure, and so it will be but kind of me to give you the opportunity of making me reparation."

Then, smarting a little under Horace Rohan's cold reception of this graciousness, she went; the long limp train of her dress trailing behind her down the staircase, with a weary and depressing sound.

In silence the twilight crept into the quiet room; whose solitary occupant paced its length slowly to and fro, the stern look fading from his face gradually, as the light faded from the summer sky. All thought and remembrance of Miss Vermont's flippancy and persistency were lost now, as his mind grasped and held a vague and floating melody. His head was raised a moment, and he had just paused beside the piano, when again an unexpected visitor entered the room, and Horace had to turn from the instrument, the half-caught melody lost in his surprise, as he met the rather abashed gaze of the young man who had entered with such an evident effort at *sang-froid.*

" Your astonishment at seeing me thus is quite natural, Mr. Rohan," he said, his eyes lowered, and his hands restless and nervous. "Three months ago, when you saw me last, I was nearly at the top of the ladder—in my own particular line—was I not? And I arrogantly enough resented a hint you offered me as to the rendering of one special verse in a song of yours, which I had just sung. I hope, if you remember it——"

"I don't," returned Horace, quietly; and at that moment a street-organ began to play under his open window, and the first faint creation of his own air was lost.

"Since then," said Rohan's visitor, glancing nervously into the quiet listening face, "times have been very hard with me. My voice has failed me through a neglected cold, and I'm very hard up indeed, Mr. Rohan."

"I'm very sorry," observed Horace, in his cool, straightforward way. "I'm hard up myself. How can I help you—again?"

"I know quite well," said his visitor, wincing at this slight reminder of previous demands, " that it is cool of me to hint at pecuniary assistance from one who has, like myself, to work for a livelihood, depending, like my own, on the caprice of the public. But you see, Mr. Rohan," he added, as Horace threw a shilling from the open window, with a shake of his head to silence the organ-grinder below, " sometimes I am tempted to give credence to the report that you are independent of the profession you choose to follow. I mean— sir " (he added the last word involuntarily, as he glanced into Horace Rohan's face), " that the fact of your publishing your songs anonymously, and seeming to care so little about their public reception; and your manners and habits, and appearance—excuse me, Mr. Rohan—and the seclusion you maintain, as well as one or two other things, have engendered the opinion, and I must acknowledge that tonight I'm tempted to endorse it."

" All right," said Rohan, carelessly.

" It seems such a shame," persisted his

visitor, touching a pile of new music which lay on the table, "that all these compositions—so greedily received by the public, and so thoroughly appreciated by us in the orchestras—should not bear your name with them down to posterity."

"None of this is what you came to say to me, Leslie," interposed Horace, with quiet indifference. "These questions affect none but myself, and you came to discuss a question which affects *you*. If I could live independently of my work, I should not work; so you can understand that I want what I earn. You, under present circumstances, want rather *more* than you earn, so—look, I have seven pounds four shillings; not one farthing more in hand or in trust, for, let report say what it will, I'm as poor a man as yourself. This we will share.—Pooh, it is not worth thanks! I know you too well to think that three pounds twelve will last you long."

The deprecated thanks were very profuse, in spite of this speech, yet Horace had no cynical smile upon his lips when he was once more left alone. The door had scarcely closed behind his visitor, when he sat down to the piano; and as he played, in the dreamy fading light, there grew a smile that was almost tender, both on his lips and in his saddened eyes.

At last, when there was scarcely light enough within the room to show this changing expression as he played on, the door was opened once again, and a gentleman entered very quietly, then, without proclaiming his presence, stood listening.

But those who live much alone are keen to detect another's presence, even without seeing or hearing; and Horace, thinking his landlady had sought him, turned his head absently as he played. But when he saw who had entered, he rose, closing the piano with fingers which were not very steady, though a moment afterwards he faced his visitor with the utmost ease.

" Rohan," this visitor said, with a laugh,

as he offered his hand, "you could not hide from me that first sensation of pride and disappointment. I felt in a moment how Ahab must have looked when he so politely greeted Elijah with the rather unnecessary interrogation, 'Hast thou found me, O mine enemy?'"

"*You* have found me," observed Horace, coolly; as he drew himself a chair opposite to his already seated visitor, and sat astride upon it, leaning with both hands upon the back of it.

"Yes, I have found you," Steven Pratman said, with a shrewd, pleased smile. "We lawyers soon find a man when we want him, and I want you. But first tell me how you are. I don't ask how you are getting on, for I feel as if I knew. Fame you refuse to accept, by keeping your works secret; and, as for your finances—why, you have only yourself to provide for."

"Only myself," assented Horace, without troubling himself to wonder why an old

friend should apparently enjoy this notion
of solitude.   "I never spend money upon
anyone else.   Why should I ?"

"And you mix in no society now," continued the lawyer, almost seeming to relish
his aggravating remarks, "being equally
too proud to join that to which you were
so long accustomed, and that into which
your present choice of profession naturally
throws you.   Pleasant, isn't it ?   As pleasant as—the Bastille."

"I can picture to myself circumstances
under which the Bastille might be pleasant
to a man," observed Horace, in a careless,
pausing way.

"But no circumstances," returned the
lawyer, uncompromisingly, "under which
a man might regret to leave it—eh ?
Rohan," he added, in sudden and unexpected earnestness, "I've not traced you,
and disturbed you here in your solitude,
only out of curiosity, or to indulge a
little characteristic quizzing.   No; I have
come to you to-night with news which will

change the whole tenor of your life. Your
proper place and position are your own
again, old fellow. The law has restored
you your birthright; and I don't believe
even you yourself will be so glad to be at
Hilton Guise once more as I shall be to
see you there."

One start Horace had given, while his
face flushed almost like a girl's; but the
next moment he was sitting again in that
indolent attitude of his, with a stillness
which in Steven Pratman's eyes had always
seemed peculiarly characteristic of him.

"I mean it," the lawyer asserted, with
a nod which was intended to be the death-
blow to all doubt. " Hilton Guise and all
your father's property are yours, dear
fellow, at last. Come, don't sit there like
a study in shadows. Do you fully understand me?"

"No."

"Then listen," Mr. Pratman continued,
wondering why Horace's manner recalled
so vividly to his memory the wretched day

when he had had to break to him the news
of his father's unjust will. " Your late
father's step-daughter, who inherited
everything under his will, has herself gone
over to the majority. She died in Nice
last Monday—she has been consumptive
for years, I find—and, like a sensible girl,
had previously made her will in proper
form, knowing that she could not live.
Poor girl ! I remember her as such a tiny
delicate child, yet such a spirited little
thing too. You recollect her ?"

" I recollect one thing," said Horace, in
haughty quietness. " She was her mother's
child."

"Yet that is the one fact which a man
might be excused for doubting," returned
Mr. Pratman, with a smile. " I found it
hard to believe even from the first; harder
still when I saw how keenly and terribly
—child as she was—she felt the injustice
done to you ; harder still when she left
home, and told me, with such real anguish
in her childish petulance, that she would

never go back to Hilton Guise. Harder
still when she ignored my wise advice to
her, on the death of her mother, to return
to take her place in her step-father's home
as his acknowledged heiress. Harder still
when, though legally possessing the magnificent estate, she coolly left it vacant,
and pursued her own humble insignificant
career. And hardest of all, Rohan, now
that she has so justly restored all to you,
in one of the humblest and most unortho-
dox of little wills, yet with all legal exact-
ness—poor girl! It is surprising to me
how a young lady, who has hitherto shown
such slight knowledge of, or respect for,
law, and with no legal relatives, should
have bequeathed so circumstantially the
property she has never claimed."

"Were you in Nice then?" questioned
Horace, with a sternness in his voice which
sounded almost cruel.

"No. I'm sorry to say the letter did
not reach me in time—by some fault, I
suppose, in the foreign offices. I was

really disappointed. If I had only heard in time, both you and I could have gone over and paid the last possible respect to the girl who so generously, though eccentrically, ignored that will; and yet so justly restored everything to you at the last."

"But the old robbery—" began Horace; then he stopped and rose, and stood beside the window in the deepening twilight, very still and grave.

"The old robbery, as you quite justly call it, Rohan," put in the lawyer, cordially, "was not hers—poor little girl!"

"Don't trouble yourself to ejaculate so many *poor girls*," remarked Horace, with an impatience which his old friend, who knew him so well, was even glad to see. "You do it to elicit pity and forbearance from me. I have neither to give."

"You know," Mr. Pratman went on, "how for a year and a half I have been advertising, and using other means to trace Evelyn Carmichael. Well, all the time she knew this, and eluded me, while she lived in the quietest and most simple way with an old schoolfellow."

"As she is dead," said Horace, quietly, " need we speak of her to-night?"

"Yes, we need," replied the lawyer, with calm persistency, "for I want you to write a few lines to the Miss Heringham who sent me these particulars, and who of course wished me to attend the funeral. For years Evelyn Carmichael has had a home with her—even for one whole year since I sent word to Miss Carmichael that the Hilton Guise property was all hers—and I can quite understand that she received untold kindness at the hands of this friend, considering how penniless she chose to be, and what a charge Evelyn must have been in her delicate health. This Miss Heringham is a girl like Evelyn herself—the very same age, I think she says, and that would be barely four-and-twenty. The two girls lived alone since the death of Miss Heringham's mother, never long residing in one place, I believe, and always seeking warm

countries, escaping English Winters and
Springs. But it was all of no avail, you
see, as Miss Carmichael died in Nice last
Monday. Now, Rohan, let us speak of
something else. Don't you want to question me as to Hilton Guise? No? Well,
certainly you will see all for yourself soon
enough now, so it's no use worrying you
with particulars. I've done all I could,
through the non-occupancy, but now I'm
delighted to think how soon my old friend
will be back in his rightful place. I expect that the welcome you will receive will
astonish you. Now, my good fellow, rouse
yourself, and come and sup with me at the
Temple to celebrate this."

"Not to-night," said Rohan, with no
cynicism at that moment in his quiet tones.
"You have brought the past back too
vividly; and I cannot quite forget the
little child who—whose death you tell me
of."

"Whose death," supplemented the lawyer, cheerily—for the life of him he could

not help saying it just then, as, in a flash of
memory, he saw the backward years of
Horace Rohan's life—" is but a tardy act
of justice."

CHAPTER III.

A WIDE and undulating park, which the great hand of Nature had made exceeding beautiful ; and, among its ancient trees, a lofty Tudor mansion, which the skilful hands of man had made so replete with comfort, and so strong and spacious, that the artistic beauty which it lacked could scarcely be deplored. Three tiers of broad, smooth terraces running along the western side of the house, and on the highest of these a gentleman waiting on this August morning very patiently, looking round, with a shrewd, gratified smile, upon the wide rich view of park and pasture land.

" The right man in the right place at last, not a doubt about that."—So Steven

Pratman spoke to himself, as he leaned his arms on the stone balustrade.— "I'm glad indeed that we have him here again, but yet I'm not quite satisfied. That intense reserve of his is unnatural at his age. Why, bless my soul, he's ten good years younger than I am, and I look upon myself as a young man still at five-and-forty! And then his avoidance of all women—he, a rich young bachelor, to whom every mother and daughter in Sussex is trying to offer a friendly hand—is absurd! It's unnatural, and riles a man like me, who looks calmly on and sees exactly how things ought to be. Here I come down to find everything guided and managed by a master-hand; works and improvements originated, of which even *I* should never have thought; the tenants benefited in every way; the labourers treated with a consideration which, at any rate, they don't deserve; the servants worshipping their taciturn master like the feudal retainers of old days; and then into the perfection of everything he comes with that disdainful, solitary way of his. I declare all my friendly plans for his own personal welfare seem—from the way he receives them—actually to *merit* the slighting derision which he so lightly and so carelessly bestows upon them. Well, my only hope is in time—baffled Nature's sweet restorer, if I may be allowed to improve an idea of Young's. Here he is."

It was not the author of the *Night Thoughts* whose approach Mr. Pratman hailed so heartily, but the Squire of Hilton Guise, who, giving his horse to a groom, walked quickly up the terrace steps to join his friend, his shoulders and his tall riding-boots covered with dust, while not a little had found a lodging-place of its own on the dark, refined face.

"You did not expect me over again so soon, I suppose?" questioned the lawyer, as the two friends shook hands. "Would it surprise you greatly to hear that I've come to Hilton this time on business that

is not yours?   But, before I go into that,
I want to hear what you have been doing
lately—something Quixotic, I'll wager.
By the way, of course you have given up
that idea of renewing Berricot's lease on
the old terms?   Why, the land is worth
half as much again as it was when your
father let it to him!"

"I know it is, and he deserves to benefit
by that."

"Why, it's not his doing!"

"Nor is it mine; so, when convenient
to you, Pratman, he is to have the lease.
Now come in to lunch, and ask me what
you choose *afterwards*."

So the meal was taken, with only pleasant friendly conversation to accompany
it.   And, even when at last the two gentlemen sauntered out again to the west
terrace, Steven Pratman seemed only to
be continuing the idle chat, when he drift-
ed skilfully into the subject Horace Rohan
always so studiously avoided.

"Only this morning I was wondering,

Rohan, whether you had ever had any reply to the letter of sympathy you sent to Miss Heringham after Evelyn Carmichael's death—the letter I had such trouble in persuading you to write."

"Reply!" repeated Horace, coldly. "It was not written to win a reply."

"You mean," laughed his friend, "that you left no loop-hole for anyone to reply to it. Well, *chacun à son goût*. But, for my part, I'm very glad to win such letters as Miss Heringham writes; even I, the rusty man of business."

"For pity's sake, Pratman," put in Horace, curtly, as the lawyer took an envelope from his pocket, "spare me the infliction of a woman's letter."

"It's not crossed," observed Mr. Pratman, with a humorous twinkle in his eyes; "there are no blots, and—on the whole— very little objectionable spelling. Still, if you have any misgivings as to your capacity for comprehending it, I will put it back into my pocket."

"Why not burn it?"

"Because I am not a confirmed and cynical old bachelor like you, Mr. Rohan. I have a vulnerable point even yet, which will answer to a woman's shy and dainty touch."

"Well?" interrogated Horace, drily, in the unexpected pause.

"Therefore I have not burned Miss Joyce Heringham's letter—yet," continued the lawyer, placidly; "and therefore I'm valiant enough to speak of it to you."

"Is there anything then," inquired Horace, stiffly, "which I can do for Miss Heringham?"

"Possibly," assented his friend. "In this letter Miss Heringham frankly expresses a wish to see the neighbourhood in which her old friend used to live; and, as she has been recommended sea air, she thinks a little sojourn here ——"

"She is welcome," said Horace, with rather fierce haste. "I will go away and leave the house to her."

"My dear fellow," cried Steven Pratman, suppressing his involuntary smile, "do you think Miss Heringham would volunteer to billet herself at Hilton Guise?"

"Then, if not, of what use can I be?"

"I don't know yet," rejoined the lawyer, good-humouredly, "but we shall see. To begin, you, of course, know nothing about Miss Heringham, not having either seen or heard from her, so your advice in a general way is all I care to elicit. But, you see, I *have* both seen her, and heard from her—I went to Nice, you know—so *I* can pretty correctly judge now of her line of conduct. She certainly would no more visit you at Hilton Guise than she would visit my bachelor-quarters in Hilton."

"Perhaps at the Rectory," suggested Horace, feeling himself called upon to suggest something in his companion's pause.

"No," returned the lawyer, with a shake of his head. "The Rabys of course are strangers to her, and she is far too independent——"

"An independent woman," observed Horace Rohan, as a casual, passing remark, "ought to be a stranger *everywhere*."

"I too think it a pity for a woman to be independent," returned Mr. Pratman, with a swift, shrewd glance into his companion's face, "because when they are entirely dependent upon *us* for everything they do and every thought they think, they are so very much more altogether charming."

"The rooms at Cliff Cottage are vacant," put in Horace, not too patiently.

"Are they? That's capital. I know Miss Heringham will be well attended to there; and she deserves to be."

"Why?" queried Horace, a little contemptuously.

"Because," returned Steven Pratman, with promptness as well as gravity, "she was very kind herself to another solitary girl."

" Did she tell you so ?"

" Really, Rohan, this is too bad," ejaculated the lawyer, genuinely vexed. "Do you think I could ever doubt it, after my visit to Nice, and after hearing what I have heard lately of the two girls' devotion to each other ? But I suppose I shall never make you believe in a wo—— About those rooms at Cliff Cottage though," he went on, with a sudden change of tone; " I'm delighted to hear they are to be had, though the situation is a very isolated one."

" The rooms are very small, if you recollect."

" All the better," returned Mr. Pratman, quite cheerily. "Miss Heringham particularly stipulates for small rooms, to suit her income, she says, which is small too."

" Yet she shared it with Evelyn Carmichael," said Rohan, involuntarily.

" Yes ; most generously. As long as Evelyn lived, I believe Miss Heringham would have given her a home."

" *Given her a home!* Given a home, in charity, to the owner of Hilton Guise! What a disjointed world it is, Steven!"

" D'ye think so?" questioned the lawyer, briskly. " I don't. Now I've one thing more to say, Rohan. If Miss Heringham comes to Cliff Cottage, I know you will do all you can to make her stay there agreeable to her."

" Rubbish! A woman will, without any one's help, make things agreeable for herself—let who will suffer."

" How you do despise them, Rohan!" exclaimed Mr. Pratman, involuntarily.

" What wonder?" said Horace, heavily.

And his friend argued no more. He even echoed the question in his own thoughts—" What wonder?"—when he looked backward through the years of Horace Rohan's life; and saw that, stronger than his youth and hope and manhood, had been the bitter sense of injury and injustice, the very weariness of which was telling upon him now.

"For," mused the lawyer to himself, "we all know how deeply the shadows sink when the waters are dark and quiet."

CHAPTER IV.

" MR. ROHAN, you are the very person I was just wishing I could see. Do walk with me to Cliff Cottage. I want to call on the young lady who is lodging there, and I should so like to have a companion. My husband went yesterday. Do come with me."

Horace Rohan had raised his hat with a smile, when the wife of his new Rector had stopped him at his own park-gates, but the smile had gone before her speech was uttered.

" I will walk with you with pleasure, if you will have me, Mrs. Raby; but not to call on any young lady, thank you."

" Oh, I hope you will!" Mrs. Raby urged,

as pleasantly as if she had not come on purpose to tempt him to pay this respect to the lonely girl of whose kindness and generosity to Evelyn Carmichael she had heard much from Mr. Pratman. "I promise you I will not stay long."

"Is not that promise rather unfair to this Miss Heringham?" inquired Horace, as he sauntered on at the lady's side.

"It is an inducement to you. If you come, your ordeal will be soon over."

"But, if I don't come, it will be still sooner over."

"My husband thought," she persisted, rather shyly, "that, though you would not go alone, you would perhaps consent to go with me."

"If anything could induce me to go at all," said Rohan, with honest coolness, "I daresay it would be your invitation; but in this case, Mrs. Raby, even that must fail."

"I don't think it will," she smiled, as they turned from the dusty highway to the narrow cliff walk. "You surely cannot have the heart to leave me?"

"I cannot," said Horace, with composure. "But evidently you intend to leave *me*, Mrs. Raby."

"I am quite sure that I ought to call to-day," responded the Rector's wife; "and, Mr. Rohan, do you know I could venture to apply the 'ought' to you too?"

"It is a flexible word," observed Horace, laughing slightly.

And then Mrs. Raby knew no further plea would avail; and so they talked of other things, until they reached the flagstaff on the point, and Cliff Cottage lay just before them.

"If you will promise me one thing, Mr. Rohan," she said then, with a new hope, "I will not again ask you to come in with me."

"Thank you," returned Horace heartily. "I will promise, of course."

"How relieved you look!" she said, with a smile. "Well, what I want you to do is

—you have made me the promise, remember—to walk home with me in half an hour's time."

"With pleasure. Where shall I meet you?"

"If I am not here, just call at the cottage door for me, please."

If it could have been courteously done just then, Horace Roban would have declined this arrangement; but Mrs. Raby, anticipating a possible refusal, adroitly hurried away, with only a smiling reminder of his promise. Half an hour's solitude was insured to him in any case, Horace thought; and so he strolled on along the cliffs, and down a rugged path to the beach, his step light and sure among the rocks, and his keen, handsome eyes traversing the far horizon. There were a few words to be exchanged with the coastguardsman, some tidings of the fisheries to hear, and the passing sails to reconnoitre. Then Horace, deep in thought, strolled back through the village, choosing the gradual

ascent to the cliff-path, almost unconsciously, because he was so deep in thought.

The little parlour at Cliff Cottage opened
to the garden by a glass door, which stood
ajar, as Horace Rohan followed the narrow
gravelled path which led straight up to it.
This was the room 'his tenants let to the
occasional visitors to Hilton, so this was
where Mrs. Raby would be waiting for him.
It was a low, old-fashioned door, and while
he rapped he lazily calculated how much
he would have to stoop, supposing Mrs.
Raby showed herself so deficient in tact as
to oblige him to enter at all.

" Come in."

Without waiting to wonder whether
this was the invitation of the Rector's wife,
and impatient at the thought of having to
go in at all, Horace Rohan stooped and
entered the tiny room. Then he looked
round him, a little vaguely, wondering
who could have spoken, because the room
seemed empty. But presently, standing
upright again, he became aware of a small

dark head, just visible over the back of a huge easy-chair which, with its back to him, was drawn up to face a little side lattice-window, wide open to the sea wind.

"I beg your pardon," began Horace, involuntarily. "I understood Mrs. Raby was here; and she had asked me to call, or——"

"Or you would not have done so? I see."

The girl who spoke to him so coolly had risen now and turned to face him; but, though Horace did not see it, she kept one hand on the arm of her chair, almost as if she needed its support.

"No; I came simply at Mrs. Raby's request," spoke Horace, in his quiet, honest way; and, though he would have given much to leave the cottage again at once, he looked so thoroughly at his ease, that the girl, who for that moment read his face most eagerly, smiled a little in her full comprehension.

"Mrs. Raby left me quite twenty

minutes ago," she said. "You must have lost count of time."

"I suppose so," returned Horace, taking out a card, and, without handing it to the new lodger at Cliff Cottage, laying it down upon the little table near her.

With an air of quiet nonchalance, the girl stooped and read the name; but Horace could not see how the soft flush rose in her cheeks as she did so, nor how her head was lifted again only when that had faded.

"Mr. Rohan," she said then, but without extending her hand, or advancing a step nearer to him, "your name is familiar to me, because your step-sister was so true a friend of mine."

Just for a moment he wondered, in his honest, manly way, whether this girl had not been a truer friend to Evelyn than Evelyn could ever have been to her; but he only answered her listlessly, as he took the seat she offered him—

"Miss Carmichael and myself were not

related at all. You must not take me on trust as a relative of your friend's."

"Very well," said Joyce Heringham. And then she took her seat again in silence, and looked out through the open window, just as if there had been no stranger present. And this stranger, curious as the proceeding was, seemed almost to forget he was a stranger there, as, in these moments of silence, he (without even once looking steadily at her) was studying intently this girl, who sat so dreamily near him, and seemed to have forgotten his presence.

She was not pretty ! He said that to himself at once, with almost a sensation of relief in his contempt. Her cheeks were too narrow and too colourless, her chin was too small, her under-lip too prominent, and her nose too thin. Still, to see her low white forehead free from the locks which had grown so wearisome to him in his professional experience, and to see the almost comical firmness and determination

of the small chin and under-lip, and the
exquisite smoothness of the white colourless skin, gave Horace unconsciously a
faint glad sensation of freshness and purity,
as if he were out among the sea breezes.

"I have heard, Miss Heringham," he
said presently, feeling it incumbent upon
himself to break this curious silence, as
she did not apparently intend to do so,
"of your kindness to my father's step-
daughter."

"Evelyn Carmichael was the dearest
friend I ever had," returned Joyce, her
voice a little tremulous, and the hands,
which had lain so utterly idle on her
black dress, folded together uneasily as
she spoke. "I would rather not speak of
her to you until I know you better—if I
ever do."

"I never shall understand," he said,
unwittingly relentless, "why she did not
claim all she inherited by my father's
will."

"No," Joyce answered, very softly, "I

think, Mr. Rohan, that—as you say—you will never understand."

"Did the will astonish her?" Horace went on, apparently forgetting that he of his own accord now pursued the subject from which he had so long recoiled; and unconscious of the unwonted pathos in his strong, clear voice.

"It pained her beyond all words," said Joyce, looking up into his eyes with a wondering, wistful look that was scarcely more than momentary. Then she spoke again, seeming less to address anyone than to breathe a thought unconsciously. "However long she had lived, the old injustice done to you—of which that will was the crowning injury —would have made her life bitter. It— it broke her heart, while she was such a girl!"

"But she could not undo the will," Horace went on, pitilessly. "So why did she not come and claim what was her own?"

"She never acknowledged that it was hers; not for one single day. She said—I have heard her say—that Mr. Rohan's leaving his property to her lay like a crime upon her; yes, I've heard her call the act a crime."

"She proved it worse than a crime—a blunder," said Horace, quoting the famous words with quiet, cutting irony.

"She never, if she had lived to be three score and ten," said Joyce, coldly ignoring his remark, "would have taken possession of Hilton Guise."

"It was too soon for you, or for her, to judge," observed Horace, gravely. "You speak from a very slight experience. She could have had no dislike to the spot; and in time——"

"If she could *ever* have come," Joyce said, steadily, "she would have come at once, instead of living with me, as a paid companion, and in lodgings"—The girl's voice grew a little hard here, as Horace was quick to notice—"She *need* have had no toil through all her frail and delicate girlhood; and she *might* have had every care and ease and luxury through her last illness; and——"

But Joyce broke off suddenly here, her voice gentle enough now; and Horace waited breathlessly a moment, fearing a flood of tears. But she only sat a minute or two utterly still, with one hand upon her eyes; and, when she dropped it and looked up again at Horace, they were even defiant, in their great effort to be courageous and calm.

"You do not answer me, Mr. Rohan?"

"You did not question me, Miss Heringham. You were only going to tell me what might have been, if my father's heiress had returned to her own house."

"Your father's heiress!" repeated Joyce, with a strange, cold smile. "Your father's heiress! I understand. Well, if *your father's heiress* had cared to return to Hilton Guise, she might have brought me here as her guest; and the rooms are"—

looking coolly round her—"larger than these, I daresay."

"Miss Heringham," said Horace, with an involuntary earnestness which surprised himself, when he heard it in his voice, "will you care to see the house that was your friend's? There is nothing there the intrinsic value or rarity of which could charm you; but—but—for her sake who owed all other home to you, perhaps you may care for it. It is changed too a great deal—I need not try to make you understand why I wished to change all I could —but the park is the same; and that at any rate is beautiful."

"Then some day," returned Joyce, in a quiet matter-of-fact way, "I will walk through it, as I have your permission."

"Then you do not care to come to the house?" His tone was a little warmer than usual, but of course Joyce was too unfamiliar with it to know that. "If you do, I will show you all there is to see."

"I can fancy you," the girl said, with a

soft, swift laugh, " not at all bored or weari-
ed—oh, no!—most conscientiously fulfilling
your task, like that old guide on the Mount
of Olives, who says so indefatigably, ' These
are the stones that cried out.' I will spare
you, Mr. Rohan."

"I don't wish to be spared," rejoined
Horace, bluntly. " Will you come ?"

" No, thank you. I will not disturb you
in your solitude there, for I, too, know what
it is to like solitude. I cannot fancy ' *ce
grand malheur de ne pouvoir être seul.*' "

" So," said Horace, with that smile of his
which was so rarely seen, " you read La
Bruyère ?"

" Were those La Bruyère's words ?" she
inquired, with well-feigned ignorance and
indolence. " I never can be sure whose
ideas I pick up. Perhaps, if you talk any
more to me, Mr. Rohan, I may pick up a
stray one of yours, to elaborate on a future
occasion. Are you not afraid now ?"

" I can easily," said Horace, colouring
duskily over his own out-spoken words,

"read that hint, Miss Heringham; but I have not been here long. A few minutes longer will make mine an orthodox call."

"And so you will have observed a conventionality which you had not intended to undergo," returned Joyce, with a quiet laughter brightening her dark eyes. "I feel so much obliged to you, Mr. Rohan. What shall we talk about? Something very conventional it ought to be."

"If," said Rohan, still stiffly, though the laughter now was gathering even in *his* grave eyes, "in this quiet spot you find you have more leisure than you provided for, and wish to choose other books, Miss Heringham, I shall be happy to lend you any."

He had made the offer as gracefully as a man could; yet, when her thanks were only a slight, silent bow, he felt at once as if he might have known beforehand that the offer was premature, and that she would naturally resent it a little.

"I suppose you are very fond of poetry," he went on presently, feeling sure, as he looked round the little room upon her books and flowers, that this was a subject on which she would talk readily.

" Only when I understand it," she said, in a simple, straightforward way. " Most poetry is quite beyond my comprehension."

" And yet," remarked Horace, wondering over the grave lips, and wishing he might fully meet her eyes, to read her meaning there, " I could fancy it a favourite study of yours."

" But my studying days were over long ago."

Again the unusual laughter shone a moment in his eyes, but he did not answer her, and there was a little silence between them. It would have been easy for him then to take his departure, yet he did not do so. As he had been lured into this call, perhaps he felt he must perform the ceremony elaborately. So he looked round the little room once more, and hazarded another observation, because his eyes fell on the open piano.

"You play, I see, Miss Heringham. Are you fond of music?" The question came very naturally, and yet her quick ears caught at once an undertone of weariness of the subject.

"How troublesome it is to find conversation suited to the feminine mind, and yet not too insignificant for you to originate, Mr. Rohan, isn't it?" she asked, with such perfect gravity upon her thin, small face that the words, whatever they had been, could have borne no sting. "I will help you. You shall not have all the catechising to pursue. I learned to play at school—experience has taught me that most girls do—and sometimes I can even yet go through a piece without many stoppages. Certainly, I very often forget what key I'm playing in, and vary it promiscuously, while the pedals are utterly beyond me; but generally I find that people say 'Thank you' when I've finished—though, of course, they look very glad. Do I sing? Is that the next question you would put to me? Yes,

I sing, but only within a very narrow compass; and most of my notes are husky.
In short, my vocal landscape is inclined
to be flat. But I've been very persever-
ing, and at last have mastered one or two
of Claribel's simplest works."

"I see one song upon your piano," said
Horace, with a slight hesitation, "which I
know. And, if you sing *that*, I must con-
tradict you, and say your compass is not
very limited."

"I see which you mean," she returned,
with a quick little nod, as if in haste to
dismiss the subject, yet speaking gently as
of something she loved, "but I sing that
song only to myself. To continue our cate-
chism," she went on, her eyes brightening
again, perhaps reflecting some inexplicable
brightness which had come into Horace
Rohan's at her last words, "I can read a
little. In fact, I have read the third volumes
of most of the novels that ever were
written; I've left off wasting my time over
the first and second, as I've found that

to be unnecessary labour. I can talk a
little sometimes; and I don't break Pris-
cian's head oftener than the average female.
Writing I don't understand. I've no one
to write to, so I never try it."

"Have you," he queried, seemingly himself taken unaware by his own question,
"really no friends, Miss Heringham."

"Only one. She is certainly the best
friend I could have, but she travels with
me always."

"Yourself," said Horace, in his quick
comprehension of the grave, harmless irony
which was new to him. And then, after a
little pause, he asked, "Do you ride, Miss
Heringham?"

"Oh, I thought I had finished!" she
cried, with a little gesture of annoyance,
yet still so gently that he caught himself
wondering if it would be possible for *any*
words of hers to sound harsh or unkind.
"I don't ride, and I have no horse. I
entertain a strictly private opinion of my
own that I should tumble off on an average

twice in every mile—but that is not the *only* reason I don't ride. Is that all? No, I never drive. The weakest little pony ever driven could run away with me at his own sweet will; but—that is not the *only* reason I never drive."

" You walk, I hope?" put in Horace, with scarcely a shade of the old haughty sarcasm in his questioning voice.

"I don't walk well," was the sedate reply. " Sometimes I think I was not properly taught, and at other times I feel convinced that only my dress is to blame; it has to be so narrow."

" Has to be?" laughed Horace.

" You don't understand, I see, Mr. Rohan. Could any woman be so lost to all sense of amalgamation as to wear a full skirt when other women tie theirs back? We might just as well be our own grandmothers at once. What a puzzled frown you wear! What is your perplexity now?"

"I could not help wondering how it was," said Horace, answering absently, but without hesitation, " that words which would sound flippant enough from most girls do not seem at all so from your lips. It is just as if—as if I listened to one of Calverley's poems sung to—the ' Marseillaise.' But you will not understand that."

" No, " returned Joyce, very slowly, as she once more raised her eyes to his face, "I do not understand. The conventional time has passed now, Mr Rohan, and you will be glad to be released."

" I am not," said Horace, abruptly; and then once more there fell a strange, inexplicable little silence between them. Joyce broke it at last, in a new quiet graceful way, as she rose from her big chair.

" Mr. Rohan, as you are not in haste to go, will you take tea with me ? Don't look surprised, please. I shall feel so very uncomfortable if you do, because I'm ignorant of what is considered conventional in English villages. I ask because if you were not here, I should have tea now—alone."

" And I shall be really grateful," replied

Horace, quite heartily, " if to-day you will take it now, and not alone. Let me ring. Yet I ought not to stay, for I remember how unmistakably you told me you liked solitude."

"So I do; don't you?" said Joyce coolly, as she crossed the room to give her orders to her landlady.

"Yes," he answered, with a rather long and steadfast gaze into her eyes, as she came back and stood near him; "but your resolute way of saying it made me fear— at least now makes me fear—" he corrected honestly, "that you are not anxious to make new friends. Else I would try——"

"Oh, don't!" she said, with an impulsive movement of both hands to her lips— such thin, delicate hands they were!

"Have you no trust in friends?" he asked, without knowing that it was the consciousness of his *own* want of trust which made his voice so almost pitifully earnest.

She read the earnestness only, and

answered with a defiant gaiety which had
no sound in it of the tears that lay so
near.

"None. I always think of the Indians
who brought Miles Standish those presents
of furs—you remember? 'Friendship
was in their looks, but in their hearts there
was hatred.'"

"What a cruel idea!" said Horace
Rohan, never guessing that he spoke to
her in real anger; and less still guessing
the reason of his own anger at such words.

"Is it?" she asked debonairly. "Perhaps so. You have *thought* it often, I
have no doubt; but then men have a right
to mistrust and suspect whom they will.
It is only from a woman's lips that the
words sound cruel and—unnatural."

"I wish I felt," said Horace, with his
old easy disdain, "that from a woman's
lips suspicion and mistrust *did* sound unnatural."

"You have found them come very
naturally, have you?" she asked. But yet

she seemed purposely to prevent his answering, by turning away from him and preparing the table for tea.

Many a time, in the after-years, did Horace Rohan look back upon that evening he had spent in the little cottage parlour, and wonder wherein had lain its subtle and engrossing charm. Long before, in his early manhood, when every house was open to his father's heir, and everywhere he was welcomed for his own sake, it had been an easy occupation to him to idle away an hour in a lady's sitting-room, though it had never been a favourite one even then. And for all the years since he had lost his trust in womanhood, he had shunned it with horror. Yet here he had lingered on and on; until the sunset flush had come softly in to remind him of how the Summer hours had sped. He did not guess it at the time, but he knew afterwards that he had had no need to constrain himself to stay. His duty would have been sufficiently performed to this

friend of Evelyn's if he had left her after
the first half-hour; and in any one of those
strange fits of silence of hers he might
most easily have done so.   Yet it was not
till the sun just touched the sea, far
beyond her little open window, that he
rose and told her that he ought to go.

" How beautiful it is !"

She was standing at the window, and
had not yet turned her eyes even to say
good-bye to him—just as if she knew that
he had even yet not actually offered his
hand, or said the last word.

From the western terrace at Hilton
Guise, Horace Rohan could see the sun set
every evening; yet now he stood and gazed
upon it from this narrow latticed window
as if he had never seen it before; wondering what was this new vague, delicious
dream which seemed to shed just such a
glory as *this* over the chill, grey, solitary
level of his own chosen life.

And Joyce watched the sunset too,
standing as motionless as he did; yet when

the last glimpse of the crimson disc was lost beyond the quiet water, and the dainty pink clouds, high above it, broke and scattered, she moved backwards a little unsteadily, and drew one hand slowly across her forehead.

"Are you so tired?" Horace asked, understanding her so little. "Did you not think it very beautiful?"

Then, quite suddenly, she hid her face upon the cushions of the great ugly easy-chair in which Horace had first found her, and cried with such intense and passionate misery that to Horace—in his ignorance—it seemed as if the slight, frail form could never live through such a storm of weeping.

"You do not know," she said, when at last, through her tears, she looked up wearily at him, as he tried and tried to soothe and comfort her; "but they were other sunsets I remember—long ago—in my childhood. And one—in Nice."

"I understand," he answered, very softly, as he laid one hand gently upon her

P 2

head. "We all have our sad memories, I suppose; and think what mine must be, when I have lived so much longer in the world than you! But it may be all the better. I may see more beauty in my sunsets now, from having so many grey and heavy scenes to look upon."

Then he took the hand she gave him within both of his, for a minute, and, before she had quite understood for what he thanked her, he was gone.

He was a man of thirty-six, hard and cold and cynical; a man who had tasted life in many aspects, and found it always pall upon and weary him; yet this evening, as he walked so slowly along the familiar road, even in his thoughts he had no contempt for the girl who had so childishly broken down before him. That morning he would have walked ten miles to avoid an introduction to her, and twice ten if he had anticipated the probability of being witness to a woman's tears; yet now there was no taint of regret upon his backward thoughts; and, strange to say, that involuntary unsubdued fit of weeping seemed to have given him just the insight he wanted into the sensitive, nervous, highly-strung temperament of the girl whose alternate fits of ironical gravity and thoughtful silence had puzzled him so much.

But, after all, he only said to himself, as he slowly mounted the terrace steps at home—

"No; I don't think I ever saw a more beautiful sunset."

CHAPTER V.

" I'VE been only three weeks in this little cottage, yet it has grown to feel as much like home as—any of those temporary dwellings in which I have spent my whole five-and-twenty years. My tiny quiet nest upon the cliffs! There is another wrench in store for me when I once more travel on."

Joyce Heringham snapped the thought abruptly, with a little spasmodic gasp, and then, catching sight of a half-opened rose growing above the garden wicket, she strolled down the narrow path, and climbed to the bar of the gate to reach it.

"I think," remarked Horace Rohan, coming up to the gate at that very moment, "that a taller person would do it more successfully, Miss Heringham."

"Well, you are taller; and, if you reach that," she said, debonairly blending the words with her greeting, "I will go and gather a spray of sweet-brier from that far corner."

A cloud fell over his face as she so quickly walked away from him, but it was scattered a minute afterwards, for he followed her with the rose in his hand, and she thanked him for it, and put it in between the buttons of her dress.

"I have come," he said, with little of the old haughtiness in his handsome, earnest face, "to tempt you to change your mind, and come to-day to Hilton Guise."

"No, oh, no!"

"To-morrow then," he pleaded, "or the next day—any day, only make me the promise to come. I can wait for the performance of the promise, if you would rather delay it."

" Yes, I would rather delay it," she said, as she took her seat on a grim little garden bench beneath an apple-tree. " I would rather delay my visit, please, for a few—years."

His thanks had been hovering on his lips, but at the last word—uttered so easily and carelessly, yet with such open indifference to his disappointment—they closed with the old scornful reticence.

" You mean this ?" he asked, presently.

" Don't people always mean what they say ?" she rejoined, with a smile, the meaning of which he, in his anger, did not stop to analyse.

So he did not answer, and there was a little resentful silence between them, which Joyce would not make even the most feeble attempt to break.

" It is a beautiful day for a canter along the Hilton Sands," said Horace, when at last he had regained his patience, turning, as he sat beside her, to look straight into her thoughtful eyes.

" Yes, I think so."

" Then will you come ?" he pleaded, with a visible effort to hide his own eager-ness because she was so calm and cold. " I will fetch the horses, and be here again within half an hour. I am sure you will enjoy it, and it will be such a favour to me. Do come."

" I have no wish for you to see me deposited upon the sand, thank you," she said, quietly, " so—— No, don't urge me, please. It wearies us both. Nothing will tempt me to go."

" If you would rather drive, it will be just as easy to me to fetch the phae-ton."

" Fetch it here ?" queried Joyce, with an astonished pucker in her forehead. " Could you not drive more easily from Hilton Guise ?"

" I could," he replied heavily, " but I do not wish to go unless you come."

" No, thank you," Joyce said again, but with that great gentleness which seemed

to take the sting from any words that
might be brusque and cold.

"I know," observed Horace, with one
last attempt, "that you are fond of walking. Will you walk to the beach this
afternoon with me, or to the woods, or
anywhere you may choose? You cannot
have seen any of our prettiest spots yet."

"Yes, I am very fond of walking. I go
for a long walk every day. To-day I went
early, and had just come back when you
found me at the gate."

"And you will not take another walk?"

"Not to-day;" and, as she spoke, her
eyes, all unconsciously, went up to where,
upon one of the nearer hills, a little chapel,
half in ruins, stood out against the clear
blue Autumn sky.

"Have you been there yet? Have you
been to St. Margaret's Chapel?" asked
Horace, following the direction of her
almost wistful gaze.

"Yes; I was there to-day."

"So early this morning! I am very

sorry. I should have liked to walk with you there. Is it not a picturesque old spot! You will like to go again, will you not?"

"No, I think not," said Joyce, with a sudden and petulant change in her manner, though with still that look of calm and purity upon her low white brow. "Picturesque, do you call it? I think those earthy graves, bound down against the wind with willow-bands, look just like mummies lying there unguarded and unheeded on the hill; and the chief things I saw among the ruins were egg-shells and chicken-bones. Picturesque! How?"

"I can remember," observed Horace, for the moment carried away to speak of a time he so rarely mentioned, "how little Ev—the child who called herself my sister —used to tempt me constantly to that spot with her; and we would sit for hours there, looking out on the wide sea view."

"Instead of on the chicken-bones and egg-shells?"

"Miss Heringham," said Horace, with a little surprise in his steadfast gaze, " do I weary you so much ?"

"You do not weary me at all," replied Joyce, while the startled gaze with which she had received his first voluntary mention of Evelyn Carmichael's childhood, melted into a smile he liked. " I was glad to hear why you cared for that grim and desolate old chapel on the hill. I was glad to feel that long ago—if only once or twice—you felt Evelyn to be in some sort a companion, child as she was."

" I felt her so many a time, and I have had no real companion since," Horace said, noticing how his tender mention of her friend had brought a new sweet light into her eyes.

" I am very glad, for I had no idea you cared for her."

" I cared for her so well that the blow was doubly hard when I lost my trust in her, as her mother's child ; and—through them—in all womanhood and girlhood for

ten years of my life. I thank Heaven now
that it was only for those ten years."

"I think," said Joyce gently, "that I
ought to tell you what only I of course
could tell; how well, in those old days,
she had cared for you; how she loved
afterwards, she said, to remember your
kindness and indulgence to a rather lonely
child."

"Thank you," returned Horace, briefly.
"Do not let us talk of her again. You
spoke of the loneliness of her childhood
just as if you could feel it. Is it because
you are lonely now?"

"I am not a child," said Joyce, suddenly rising and moving towards the cottage;
"and I have never been disappointed in a
friend. It is impossible to compare the
cases."

"I wish it were easier to understand
you, Miss Heringham," observed Rohan,
in his grave direct way, as he walked on
beside her. "Sometimes you drive me
back in every word I say, and then some-

times I chance to see you so different—I
beg your pardon, but it really does seem
as if it were only by *chance* that I ever see
you different—kind I mean, and so very
pleasant ; so exactly what your name
means."

"My name !" she echoed, looking without a smile into his face. "What does my
name mean ?"

"*Pleasant*," he said, lingering over the
word. "Did you not know that that was
the meaning of *Joyce ?*"

It was as impossible for him to hide the
tenderness which came into that first utterance of her name, as it was for her to hide
the soft fleeting blush which rose in her
white cheeks at his utterance of it. Yet
she made a quick and childish endeavour
to hide it when too late, for she bent her
head against the fresh sea breeze, and
actually ran up the narrow path, and into
the little parlour—Horace following her.

"You come in uninvited, Mr. Rohan,"
she said, leaning on the back of the big

easy-chair, and facing him with a frown which apparently did not strike him as very forbidding. "I consider it a very unfeeling reminder that the rooms are really yours."

"No, you do not," returned Rohan promptly. "You know quite well why I come. You know that there is no other spot on earth where I feel as I feel here. Heaven knows that there is little that is good in me, Joyce, but what there is has come forth only in your presence, and only at your touch. So, to win the only happiness I know, I haunt your room; and wait for you; and long for you; and," he added, with a flash of laughing honesty, " get nipped and scolded and humiliated for my pains."

"And do you like that?" inquired Joyce, with gravest anxiety.

"There are one or two things which I should like to amend for my own sake. For instance, if you would just occasionally grant a request of mine. You have never even yet sung me one single verse."

"*Even yet!*" she echoed, with puckered lips. "You insinuate that our acquaintance has been of endless date."

"Miss Heringham," he pleaded, as he took one of his own songs from the piano, "if you would sing this to me it would be such a treat."

"I cannot," she said, very low, as, still leaning on the back of the chair, she dropped her head upon her folded hands. "It was—Evelyn's song."

"But you have sung it since," he urged; "and indeed it will be easier to you every time. Do give me this great pleasure. Do open your heart a little to a new friend, though it is so leal to the old one."

"No new one can ever take the place of —my first best friend," she said, lifting a face that looked almost bright, though it was a little paler than its wont.

"I do not ask to take her place. I want a very different one; only your heart

seems closed to all other—closed, I mean,
to *love* by the seal of this past friendship."

"Leave me the seal unbroken, please,"
Joyce entreated, very gently.

"But how unfair it is!" cried Horace,
almost wrathfully, though his heart beat
with passionate tenderness. "You try
always to send me from you. You avoid
my companionship; you will not visit my
house or my friends. You will go with
me nowhere; you will let me do nothing
to give you pleasure; yet, if you only
knew——"

"You mean if I only knew how disagree-
able it made me, I should not do it; but I
do know, and still I do it."

"Why do you always stop me?" Rohan
asked, still angrily perplexed; yet with an
intense yearning to fold his arms about
the fragile girl, and guard and cherish her
in spite of herself. "Is yours to be a
lonely life for ever, and no man to have
the power of——"

"My life is very full of enjoyment and amusement, and everything nice, Mr. Rohan. You cannot imagine how very comfortable it is."

"Joyce," he cried, in a voice of intense longing, "why are your words so cruel to me, and yet your voice and eyes are not? Oh, my child, so well beloved, when shall I understand you?"

"Never," Joyce said, with a suspicious sound of tears in her clear gay voice. "I am a study far above your comprehension, Mr. Rohan. Would you kindly ring that bell for me? I do so want my lunch."

CHAPTER VI.

MR. PRATMAN had read his evening letters; had given final directions to his clerks, and, having left his business affairs in smoothest train, waited only for his horse; for he intended to ride round to Hilton Guise, that he might see Horace Rohan before going up to town by that night's mail.

"Rohan might even be going to London himself," mused the lawyer, "and, if so, it would be pleasant for us to travel together. I hope so, for it would betoken a possible, and a decidedly pleasant, change in his arrangements. There has been change enough in himself lately. The next

change I want to see is in his establish-
ment, and hers—poor little girl!"

The lawyer had mounted now, and was
riding slowly along the streets of the quiet
little town, greeting almost everyone he
met, yet continuing his thoughts unbroken
through it all, as long training had taught
him to do.

"Poor little girl!—though I daresay she
would not thank me for compassionating
her, or indeed for using that diminutive,
as if she were a child. She seems so too
sometimes, reminding me even of that
silent little step-child of the old Squire's,
who used to be always wandering away
with Horace, and was as shy and wild to
me as a young fawn—poor child! It was
a broken life, I fear, and it puzzles and
pains one, too, to think how much worse it
might have been but for this Miss Heringham, who certainly—if one might settle
these affairs—deserves in return a less
isolated life for herself."

A long pause ensued, and the lawyer's

thoughts were scattered, while he passed through a narrow bustling street on the outskirts of the town; but, when he was out on the wide and smooth highway, still riding slowly, he took up the train of thought again unchanged.

"A strange girl, too; one I am never thoroughly sure of in her moods, and yet one I could trust through all, as having so much sterling good below. No; I do not wonder at Rohan's heart being touched at last. Touched!"—with a laugh—"it is hopelessly and irremediably captured! Those women-haters are terribly intense and tenacious lovers when they do at last succumb to one of the contemned sex. I always guessed how it might be with Rohan. Indeed I have had this very situation before me. Didn't I always in silence dissent from those gloomy tales people repeated, of the hopelessness of Horace Rohan's ever changing his life, of his confirmed horror of marriage, and his persistent avoidance of the other sex?

Ah, I saw through it all, though I could
say nothing! I had my shrewd opinion
that some day Horace Rohan would not
only choose one of the women he seemed
to despise, but would love her as a man
ought to love—one woman only, and one
for ever. My only mistake," he went on,
with a little smile, which there was no
one to wonder over, "has been that I
fancied he would be ensnared by beauty;
a downright mistake, and I was thoroughly
out there. Miss Heringham has no claim
to real beauty, not a bit, though I have
seen many a beautiful face with less charm
than hers has, for even *I* enjoy being
puzzled over its perpetual changes—first
disdain upon her lips, then fun, then
childlike wistful earnestness; and all the
while that calm about her, and that purity
upon her brow, which seem to me the
essence of womanliness—if I may say so.
What a sweet and soothing companion she
could be for a man's life, and yet never
an inanimate one! Still it has not been

beauty which first captivated Rohan, nor was it gratitude, as it might possibly have been, for he never felt—as far as I could make out—in any way indebted personally to Miss Heringham for her kindness to the late Mrs. Rohan's child. No; Nature seems to have done it in some easy natural way of her own," decided Mr. Pratman, drawing his horse up to the hedge to look over into Rohan's model farm, "and has quite gently and imperceptibly, however suddenly, effected this change in Horace which it does one infinite good to see— except—except," he went on, letting his horse walk slowly to the park gates, " when there enters one's head just the faint possibility of her refusing him. By all that's miserable, I cannot, even by myself here, bear to allow the possibility of it ! I dare not actually—seasoned old on-looker as I am—picture to myself what *that* would make of Rohan. He has put heart and soul—bah, what do I know about it?"

He purposely avoided pursuing this

thought as he rode through the park, glancing continually around him with a very perfect and evident approval of all he saw. But a disappointment met him when he reached the house, for Mr. Rohan was not at home. So Steven Pratman, with the privilege of an old friend, took a seat by the library fire, and read himself promptly and comfortably into a placid afternoon nap.

*   *   *   *   *   *

It had become such a usual thing for the landlady of Cliff Cottage to see the Squire stroll up to her little garden gate, that she rarely now stopped in her work to watch him; else upon this wintry morning she would have hurried out at once, to save him the unnecessary trouble of coming on into the parlour while her lodger was out. But Horace evidently thought it no trouble to come up the narrow path to Joyce's room, and when his summons upon the open door received no answer, he un-

covered and entered the room, as he had
so often done before. It was no new thing
at all for him to find the little parlour
empty, and say he would await Joyce's
entrance, or, finding she was out upon the
cliffs, to hasten on to meet her there.
But to-day he stood irresolute. He had
been so wholly engrossed by his thoughts
of her that he seemed now suddenly to
feel her absence like an unexpected blow.
Yet was not the little room filled with
pleasant tokens of her presence, and crowd-
ed for him with sweetest memories ? There,
as always, facing the open window, was
the big chair in which he had first seen her,
and from which perhaps she watched the
sunset still, as she had watched it on that
night with him. There lay her brushes
and her palette beside an unfinished sketch.
There lay her open book, its pages ruthless-
ly kept down by a tilted letter-weight.
There was the pretty little work-basket,
full to overflowing; and there upon the
desk of the piano a song stood open at the

last page, as if it had been lately sung through.

When Horace's eyes fell on this, their tenderness deepened, as well as their gladness, for this was one of his own songs, and the words were the utterance of a girl's undying love. Would Joyce ever sing it to him? And would he some day be able to tell her whose melody it was? Should he ever talk to her of how the harmonies came to him in his great loneliness, and were his only companions? Would she ever let him play to her the old memories of those solitary times, with now the fuller, deeper harmony of those perfect days? And would she ever answer in the words of his own song, and make his life one long and glad rejoicing?

"Mr. Rohan, sir, I beg your pardon."

The woman of the house had come in to make up the parlour fire, but she stopped when she saw her landlord standing there so quietly before it.

"Miss Erringham's out, sir," she explained, after Mr. Rohan's greeting, " and, I'm very sorry to say it, in this nasty bleak east wind too, coz Edwart Morgin has jest told me he see'd her goin' up to St. Margit's Chapel. What 'ud tempt her there I can't for the life of me make out, sech a day as this, an' all the winds at once blowin' right straight on St. Margit's, as I made free to tell her."

" But she was not much impressed by that view of the matter, I suppose ?" said Mr. Rohan, with a half-smile, as he prepared to leave.

" It seems to me, sir," continued the woman, looking anxiously up at the Squire, " as she goes up there to fret for that friend she lost. I mark she never goes when she seems well an' cheerful, an' I'm sure, startin' off this mornin', she didn't look fit for anythin'—after cryin' as she did too. I wouldn't tell anyone else, sir, only you, coz you know her so well, an' might get her to go cheerfuller ways than up to St. Margit's."

"I will," said Horace briefly; and then, with little evidence of either the haste or the anxiety he felt, he spoke a few kindly words to his cottage tenant, and started to follow Joyce Heringham's wandering steps.

There was but slight difficulty for him in climbing the little sea-side hill, yet he keenly felt how unwise and even dangerous it must have been for Joyce to breast the strong and cutting wind. And so well he loved her, that all the time he hoped he should not find her there, even though his heart was filled with longing for her.

But, when he had reached the top of the hill, and climbed the broken wall which ran round the little graveyard, he saw her at once, as she stood against the crumbling porch, looking out to sea, and buried in a long, long thought.

And, when he saw her thus; so sad, so pale, so small and weak, so utterly alone in this cheerless, isolated spot; his love rose in a strong and mighty tide, and swept before it all his old doubts and fears, and all his past unwillingness to startle her.

"My love !" he cried, taking her weak white hands in his. And then he could say no more, because his heart was so full, as he looked into her beautiful, awakening eyes.

* * * * * *

"Joyce, my darling, why should you speak so—trying to break your own heart as well as mine? You made me happy beyond words by that first whisper that you loved me; yet now—— But these words are all in vain, my cherished little love, for you can never call back that one delicious confession, and I am too strong to let you escape me ever again."

"Had we not better go?" whispered Joyce, with a strange and sudden trembling. "You came to fetch me home, you said, and we have been among these ruins a long, long time, haven't we?"

"A long, long time, counting by the happy years it has prepared for me,"

Horace said, kissing her with infinite
tenderness, as he wrapped her furs more
closely about her; "but it has passed like
a flying moment with me. Tell me, Joyce,
just tell me once again, that you are happy
—though not with such happiness as mine,
dear love. I know how impossible that
would be, and I am even glad to know it, for
I would not think your life had been one
of wrong and disappointment such as
mine. My darling, do not look so pained
and troubled now. For every sorrow that
my life has held, this one hour has more
than recompensed me. And to think of
what it will be from this day!"

"No, no," faltered Joyce, with unsteady
lips; "you must forget what we have said.
You took me by surprise, and you do not
know—we neither of us know each other
yet."

"Don't we, my sweet?" he cried, with
happy laughter in his voice. "Then we
can study each other all through the bliss-
ful years we shall spend together."

"If you knew me better—" she persisted, with bowed head.

"I should only love you better," he
laughed, putting her hand within his arm,
and holding it there as if he felt how
thoroughly it belonged to him; "and that
seems to me at this moment an utter im-
possibility. Don't shrink from me, my
love. Let me feel you close beside me, as
if you knew your lonely days were over;
and as if it were as natural for you to
accept my strong protection now as it is
for me to guard and love and cherish you.
Joyce, little Joyce, why do you tremble
so? Does my love weary you in its great
strength and obstinacy? I am so unused
to being happy that I ought to have tried
to control——"

"I too," she interposed, looking up at
him at last with eyes that were truthful
through their tears, and lips that were quite
steady now, "am unused to being happy;
but the most precious gift the world could
give me is your love, Horace."

" My darling," he said, simply; and that spot within the gloomy walls was bright and fair as Paradise to him just then. " My love, the happiness which is to come will be twofold for us both. Come and let us picture it, as we walk home toge- ther; for, though I must love this spot for ever, I dare not keep you longer here, my sweet white lily."

But, though he tried so earnestly, as they walked together, to win her to talk of her love, or to join in his bright fore- casting of their future, it was but of little avail. Yet, though her silence puzzled him, it could not hurt him, for those words of hers, whispered among the ruins, shone brilliantly for him before all other memories.

"I shall run up to London for a few days, my darling "—they were parting now in Joyce's little sitting-room, and while he spoke Horace held both her hands in his, and looked down into her eyes with untold love and tenderness—" to arrange about the preparing of Hilton Guise for my wife. It shall be made as beautiful as man's hands can make it, love, before you come—and whilst we are enjoying ourselves elsewhere. Then, when I take you there, what a perfect home it will be! Don't keep me long, Joyce. We have nothing to wait for, have we? Though I feel as if my life had only begun to-day, you can see plainly, dear, that half my years are gone; so do not let us waste one day of the time that we may spend together. I shall take my little wife with such pride and such delight to the places we have talked of in this little room of hers—I was always trying to find out the spots you would love best, Joyce, and treasuring in my mind the thought that we should go to them together, we two alone—and she will never again see me a cold, morose, distrustful man, as I have been for years."

"And she herself?" questioned Joyce, smiling wistfully.

"She herself? Ah, love, I cannot tell!
But there is no such change that happiness
can make in *you*. You were never hard
and cynical. You never lived an isolated
life. How often and often I have wondered over your goodness to Evelyn, and
wished I could tell you——"

"Hush! Please, hush!" whispered Joyce,
her low white forehead drawn with pain.
"I cannot bear you to speak of Evelyn
just yet."

"I will not, dear," he said, with a long,
gentle kiss. "I will speak of nothing
that in any way distresses you. What a
tender heart it is that has been given me
to-day!"

"Horace," she breathed, very low, "I
never tempted you to love me—did I? I
—I tried to—to prevent it. Oh, Horace,
I wish you saw the faults in me! I wish
you knew how many faults I have. When
you do—oh, in the years to come, when
you know it—remember how I loved you—
and—have patience with me!"

But, for all answer, he hid the sorrowful, pleading eyes upon his breast, because he dared not let her see his own.

* * * * * *

"Never was more rejoiced in my life, Rohan."

Horace had found the lawyer still placidly awaiting his return in the library at Hilton Guise, and had by degrees, urged on by the skilful questioning of his old friend, told him of his acceptance by Joyce Heringham.

"And are you not surprised, Steven?" he asked, unconscious of the new ring of happiness in his voice.

"Surprised?" echoed the lawyer, most cleverly veiling the fact that Horace had brought him exactly the tidings he had been expecting. "Well, not entirely. A man in love partakes a good deal of the ostrich, you know, and we on-lookers see a little more than he guesses. Then you will not come up with me to-night?"

"No, I think not, as I did not tell Joyce

R 2

I should. To-morrow night will be soon enough, and, as I shall get quickly through my business, I may be able to return with you this week. Why do you laugh, man? You never see a *real* joke, and yet over the dullest idea in Christendom you will laugh like a young hyena."

"Exactly," rejoined the man of law, rubbing his soft white hands together. "That is my habit. I always *did* enjoy the dullest idea in Christendom. Still I hope you are not too dull to dine to-day.

CHAPTER VII.

SUCH a gusty and wet November afternoon was it that Joyce Heringham
hastened almost nervously to close the
shutters, to draw the curtains over her
little latticed windows, and to light the
lamp and stir the fire into a blaze. Then
she stood still upon the rug, looking down
into the fire, in that thoughtful intense
stillness which seemed so essentially to
belong to her. A very pretty picture the
girl made, so small and quaint and bright
herself, and with such small and quaint
and bright surroundings. This day Horace
was to return from London; and was it
not quite possible that he would come to
the cottage? So now and then she glanced
full longingly at the closed and shuttered

door which led into the garden, and now
and then there broke from her lips a happy
snatch of song.

But when he came at last, it was not
through the familiar garden door, because
he would not bring the cutting evening
wind into her presence ; and so she did
not turn to meet him, fancying the opening of the kitchen door was only to admit
her landlady.

" Joyce, dear love," he said, joining her
upon the rug, and drawing her closely to
his side, " this is a moment to gladden a
man's heart indeed. Surely I was hidden
somewhere in that long thought of yours ?
Surely it touched me, love, however far
away you may have fancied me just
then ?"

" It was only of you," she confessed,
whispering the truth in her surprise.
" Just then my heart held no one else."
Then, as she read the delight that this confession gave him, she went on gravely, as
they still stood in the bright, caressing fire-

light, "If you are so glad of such a little thing, Horace, how are you to bear the great surprise I have in store for you—which is that I am invited to stay for a week or two at the Rectory?"

"A week or two! Only a week or two! My love, how good you are!"

"How?" faltered Joyce, her face growing a little paler even than its wont. ·

"Because, my darling, they will keep you at the Rectory until our marriage-day. They will consent to your leaving them only when *I* take you. They will welcome Joyce Heringham with the greatest delight, but they will part only with Joyce Rohan."

"Joyce—Rohan," said the girl, in a curiously sad, disheartened voice. "I do not like those names together, Horace."

"I do," he declared, with the heartiest content, looking laughingly into the shy eyes; "and I think 'a week or two' is, as you say, quite long enough for you to keep me waiting before you try it. *Joyce*

Rohan! It does not sound quite so strange to me as it does to you, love, for I have uttered it a hundred times to myself, in hope and longing."

"Please, please do not utter it again," she pleaded; then—with an unexpected change of tone and expression—"Shall we have tea, or don't you care for it?"

" Of course I don't care for it. What man in his senses would care to be waited upon by the little hands which he has walked so many a mile just for the sake of touching? What man of intelligence would care to be talked to by the girl whose voice is the only music——"

" Then will you ring, please?"

" I have a hundred things to tell you, Joyce," he said, as he drew the table to the fire and sat beside her while she poured the tea. "You have no idea, my little unimaginative love, what grand improvements we are going to have at Hilton Guise."

"Is it in a very dilapidated condition

then at present?" inquired Joyce, very much engrossed it seemed upon what she was doing. "Does it need so very much repairing?"

"You nipping child, it needs not an atom of repairing; only an immense amount of beautifying to make it worthy of its mistress."

"Who is she?"

"Do you know, Joyce, I feel actually glad now of what has lately caused me many a mortification," he went on, with a smile; "that you have never yet seen the old house. Oh, the pleasure of that first day, when I take my darling over her new home!"

"All over it?" questioned Joyce, with a pucker in her straight and delicate eyebrows. "How tired she will be!"

"Will she? Then I will carry her, for she is but a mite amongst women."

"And has she no sense? Will she allow you to treat her with such irreverence?"

"She will allow one thing," Rohan said, taking the grave face between his gentle hands and kissing it. "On that day, at any rate, she will allow it—that she is precious to her husband beyond all words."

"Will you care for a second cup, Horace? Please to remember you are at a meal."

Half an hour afterwards, when the tray had been taken away, Joyce took up her sewing, and sat down beside the lamp; but Horace gently drew the work from her fingers.

"To-night," he said, "you are going at last to grant my old request. Joyce, my darling, surely at last you will sing to me —and sing the song I choose?"

"Not that; not that, please," she entreated, as he took up the passionate, pathetic love-song which he himself had written. "I—I—think that is such a difficult song to sing. Why do you choose it?"

"Because, strange to say," he answered,

quietly, " I knew the man who composed
it ; and I should like to see how you, my
darling, interpret this one sad thought of
his."

"He must have been very unhappy
when he wrote that," Joyce said, sitting
quite still with idle hands.

"He was, dear. It was then I chanced
to know him, and he was most unhappy.
A man with no hope beyond the success of
his last song, no aim beyond the earning
of his daily bread, no friend except an idle
lounger here and there, who, by some in-
scrutable error, sought for his patronage.
What a life it—— Darling, why are
your eyes so sad and compassionate ? The
man, as I knew him then, did not deserve
any sympathy of yours ; and now everything is changed for him—I believe."

"How ?" asked Joyce, still without
joining him at the piano.

"How ! I cannot tell you how, my
love, for, if I did, you could not really
understand. You would say I exaggerated

if I tried to compare his present hopes and ambitions with those which were all he cared for when I knew him in London. Of course you would, for what can you understand, my gentle little girl, of such a marred and broken life ? Now will you sing the song for me ?"

She rose slowly, and took her seat at the piano, playing softly then, and prolonging the symphony as if she dreaded its conclusion. Horace did not hasten her. Sitting almost behind her, and shading his eyes with his hand, he waited. And when the song was ended, and she turned and took his hand down of her own accord, she saw *why* he had hidden his eyes.

"It is too sad," she said, rising hastily. "No man should compose such sorrowful airs. The melody might have been just as beautiful if hope had been its key-note instead of—of—hopelessness."

"The man *was* hopeless," said Horace, absently taking the seat she had vacated ;

"but—could it really have been the same air, Joyce, if its despondency had turned to joy? May I try?—now that I know what joy is! Listen!"

She listened, standing with her hand upon his chair, and he, ignoring both words and accompaniment, wreathed the air in such bright changing harmonies, and varied the tune so fancifully, that under his master-hand the air grew almost jubilant amongst its full impassioned chords.

And when quite suddenly, even in the middle of a bar, he lifted his hands with a laugh, and imprisoned hers, she whispered, as she laid her ips gently on his forehead—

"I know who wrote the song, Horace; I know without a word from you. Oh, my love, tell me that the hopelessness has passed, and that *this* is how you would play your love-song now? Hush, Horace, do not tell me of those past days! Never tell me; I—I could not bear it. It is a strange fancy I know, but in our happy present we can afford to lose the past, and—need not touch the future."

" Our future !" he echoed, with untold gladness. "I could talk of *that* through every hour of every day; the future which begins from that hour when we meet each other in the quiet little church over there —My love, why do you shiver? It shall be as warm that morning as this dear little room of yours. And from that hour, I say —no need to turn away, my shy little love —from that hour you cannot prevent my telling you, as often as I choose, how dearly and how faithfully I love you."

CHAPTER VIII.

THOUGH the Squire's wedding was to be unannounced, and, so to speak, a strictly private one, it seemed to Joyce that she was the centre of a dense crowd, all the way across the Rectory lawn and up the churchyard path, as she walked leaning upon the Rector's arm, with snowdrops scattered on the carpet at her feet. And then within the church it was all like a beautiful dream. A dream of leaves, and flowers, and gay forms and happy faces; with only one thing real, only one form and face quite clear and distinct before her, from the moment Horace met her with the delight and pride which he never tried to hide, and with the warm and steadfast love-light in his eyes. And when the people, speaking of her, said how pretty she looked, and how happy now, in spite of her nervous shyness, they said too, a little wonderingly, that, if she had been the greatest beauty in the land, the Squire could not have looked more proud of her.

At the quaint little flower-decked altar, Horace Rohan and Joyce Heringham had been made man and wife; and now, among a little group of friends, they stood in the small and rather over-heated vestry, while the register was opened for the concluding rites to be performed.

"This is the end, love," Horace whispered, with a smile, as he put a pen into his wife's hand, "and we shall both be glad. I want you all to myself again, and you— It is my fault that the air is oppressive here, dear. I gave such particular orders that the church was to be warm, because one day you shivered at the very thought of it. Now, love."

"Yes," she said, absently, but, instead

of looking down upon the open page, she only looked up into his face, with a strange, wistful, silent gaze.

"Your maiden name, Joyce," said the Rector's wife, coming up to the table ; and standing at the bride's left hand, with a little air of encouragement and reassurance.

"My maiden name—my own ?" Joyce questioned, but still without turning her eyes from the handsome, rather amused face of her husband, as he waited close beside her, his own fingers touching hers as they held the pen.

"Your old name, darling, for the last time. If you feel faint in here, I will have the book carried out. If not, write it quickly, dear little wife, and then we are at liberty to go."

"I will write it now," she said, in a strange, intense whisper. "Where am I to write ?"

"On this line, dear," responded Mrs. Raby, wondering over the question, because she had more than once laid her own finger on the spot. But Horace had answered too, by taking his bride's hand within his own, and guiding it to the blank line.

"Now," he said, releasing the small white fingers.

And still she paused, while her hand shook a little as it lay upon the book.

"Does it seem so strange to you, my love, to write the old name for the last time?" whispered Rohan, still hovering about the slender, white-clad figure. "Come, it is not very long, and this close room is making you so sadly pale. Suppose I have to write it for you, and then Pratman tells us some day that our marriage was not legal?"

"Would he?" questioned Joyce, just above her breath; but not glancing at her husband's friend, who stood so near them. "Would he say so—if I did not sign—or signed—wrongly?"

"Of course he would, dear love," laughed Horace, touching her fingers once again to hasten her.

"I see," she said, with quickening breath and wide and troubled eyes. And then she bent her head and wrote—

"EVELYN CARMICHAEL."

They were only two words, and as she began to write her husband had been looking proudly and tenderly down upon her. Yet, when she dropped her pen and lifted her face to his, fixing her eyes yearningly upon it, as if she forgot everyone save him—as if she felt his presence only, and cared for nothing in the world beyond his smile of pardon—she saw with what an awful suddenness the smile of pride and fondness had died. She saw how cold and rigid his face had grown, while that terrible pallor spread slowly to the tightened lips. And there broke from her a pitiful cry, which no consciousness of strangers round them could have power to suppress—

s 2

" Oh, Horace !"

Slowly he stepped back from her at the
sound of her voice, still looking down upon
her as if he too saw no one else.   But, oh,
with such intensity of scorn as well as
anguish !

"Oh! Horace, pity me!"   But the cry
for pardon never seemed even to reach
him.

So they stood facing each other, as if,
for either, the world held no one else ; and
one by one the strangers who had come to
rejoice with them turned silently and sadly from the room.

And, passing the bride, it was to the
bridegroom's side that the Rector's wife
crept with such true compassion on her
face ; though the girl's slight form tottered
in very weakness, as she leaned against the
table with both hands, in real need of its
support.

"Horace," Evelyn said at last, her lips
dry and stiff as the low whisper passed
them, "it was Joyce Heringhan who died;

and I—I did it for—the best. Oh, Horace, let me tell you all. You—alone! You are—my husband, and—you ought to listen. Will you, Horace? Will you listen? Oh, this is—killing me!"

"You have nothing *more* to tell me," said Horace then, the words falling heavily from his lips, while still his eyes rested on the girlish form, in a very intensity of anger and despair. "You have told me—enough. You have lied skilfully. As skilfully "—the words passed his teeth almost with a hiss—"as only a woman can. Even your mother," he went on, the veins rising in his forehead, and his lips white with rage, "could not lie more ingeniously, or befool a man more utterly than—*you!*"

"Horace," she pleaded from her breaking heart, "just let me tell you of that one night—in Nice, when the temptation overmastered me. It—it was in the sunset. I remember trying to tell you of it —once. I know how wicked I was—I always knew it. I tried to prevent your caring for me. You—you knew I did. I would not have come—here, if I had ever guessed that when I came, you—might care for me. I thought you never would love any woman. I thought so, Horace. Oh, believe me!"

"I have believed you far too long," he said, still strangely, pitifully motionless, while the veins rose higher in his weary, anguished face. "There is no need of more deception. You can go now, Miss Carmichael, to your own home—to Hilton Guise. I am glad to think it—it has been prepared for your reception, though I—had no right to do it. You are its mistress indeed! Go and reign and govern, as you knew you—ought to do."

"If I had known *that*," cried Evelyn, with a momentary feverish flash of daring, "I could have gone long ago—long ago!"

"And until the old house crumbles into dust I—will never disturb you there."

"Oh, Horace, listen to my one excuse!"

But her words could not reach his brain, while such a storm of passions surged about him. And as they passed him by unheard, he bent a little, and—looking still into her face—*laughed.*

"Evelyn Carmichael, why do you stay here? You forget that my father's house is yours, and—ready for you. It has been yours for a long time, justly yours; not left to *you* by a false will—forged—by—a dying girl."

"No! No!" cried Evelyn, clasping her head between her hands, with a perfect agony of contradiction on her face. "It was not Joyce who did it; it was I—only I! She thought she signed her own will only—her own innocent kind will, in which she left me all she had. But she signed twice; and—and *I* did all the rest. It was I who deceived, not she—never Joyce! And even you, Horace, shall say no words of blame of *her.*"

"*Joyce—Joyce——*" He repeated the

name absently, with such a smile upon his stiff white lips, that his wife covered her eyes and shuddered when she saw it. " What need have we to speak of the dead —here, where there has been—a wedding. A broken wedding, and—no wife ?"

"Hush, Horace ! Oh, in pity hush !" she cried, the words panting from her lips, and her breast heaving with stifled sobs. " Am I not your wife ?"

"My wife ? Oh, no !" He said it smiling, with a fierce grasp at his failing energies, and a defiance of the torture that he suffered. " No, no wife of mine—but Miss Carmichael of Hilton Guise. Steven, let the people welcome her—as you told her they would. Raby, won't your smiling guests rejoice to see my father's heiress reinstated in—her rights ? They will pity her for having been kept out of them so long, of course ; and they'll tell her she makes a wise—and good—and pretty—mistress of the old house. For a hundred years—they will say—it has not had so sweet and bright a one—Fool! I've told her those same lies myself, many a time. · She taught me to lie. She was a true woman in that. Call her carriage, Steven—the new carriage which she liked so much—and let them take her back in state. She has never seen the old house yet, and there are—one or two things which she—will like. What's this?"

The question, in its terrible suddenness, and yet its ringing scorn, was still quite quietly uttered, as Evelyn fell upon the floor beside him, in an agony of weeping.

" There is no need for *you* to cry," he said. ,"You are a stranger to me, and—to Joyce. I am going back—to my old life. Why do you not go to yours? They are waiting for you now, and Raby wants—to close the church. It is over at last—my wife's funeral—poor Joyce! Raby, why are you shutting out the light?"

*   *   *   *   *   *

" This," mused the Rector to himself, as,

in a nameless fear, they watched the hurrying of this mental darkness, " will be a lifelong separation."

CHAPTER IX.

"ROHAN, for Heaven's sake reconsider such a decision as this! To go to America, from impulse, at such a crisis!"

"There has been no *impulse* in the question. The decision was arrived at slowly—you can never guess *how* slowly, Steven, till you know what days and nights I have spent since——"

"I can guess," Mr. Pratman put in, hurriedly intercepting the conclusion of the reply; and turning to avoid the fierce, straight gaze of Horace Rohan's eyes. "But I cannot understand, or sympathise with, this resolution of yours. I will not say anything about my own grief at losing my old friend, for of course I am not discussing my own affairs or feelings. But, to speak only of yourself, it is such an—an uncomfortable plan."

The lawyer had intended to use far more forcible words, but somehow it happened that, when he looked into his friend's haggard, restless face, his thoughts fled so painfully back over the strange and miserable past, that he lost the words which were generally so ready.

"Why is it an uncomfortable plan?" asked Horace, in the rapid, absent way in which he had spoken throughout this long and painful interview; and with a brief, keen-edged laugh which made Mr. Pratman more ill at ease than any words that could have been uttered. "There is room in America for another man, I daresay. Probably a market for songs too— though so far," he added, with a slight faltering in the bitter, cynical tone, "I have not been able to put two notes together without jarring discords—such vile, yelling, fiendish discords!"

"Horace," inquired his old friend, lowering his eyes, whilst Rohan's gaze, hot and fierce and passionate, went beyond him into far-off space, "are your nights still what they were, dear fellow, or do you sleep?"

"*Sleep!*" echoed Horace, with again that swift, unmirthful laugh. "I forget what it is like. The very word has a strange sound to me. Sleep? Sleep? I cannot remember when the nights were *not* eternal hours of darkness, thronged with words and cries and laughter. Old words that had no horror in them—once; and laughter that I could join in—once. And—and—above all, cries—clear and shrill, and lasting interminably. Such darkness as this, haunted by *one*—— Sleep, do you call it? Then God grant that in that other country I may never sleep again!"

"Horace," said his old friend, laying

one hand upon his shoulder; moved as such
a man, in his wide and varied experience
of human nature, is seldom moved, "forgive me for what I am going to say. We
have been friends too long for us to mistake each other now, or—or for us to hesi-
tate to speak the truth to each other.
Horace, dear fellow, I can understand this
wish of yours to go away. I can understand what these terrible six weeks have
been to you since your wedding day——
You may start from me as you will, but I
must speak out this once. I know, I say,
what these weeks have been to you—the
days of labour, dazed, bewildered labour,
which have brought no result; and the
nights of feverish agony. I can see what
these have left the man who was so strong
and happy and so trustful then; and I do
not wonder that they have changed him
so. But I see too that the very keenness
of his suffering shows the tender heart
below; and—and, Horace, dear, dear fellow, listen just once to the softened plead-

ing tones of that angel-whisper; and—as you yourself will need to be forgiven—forgive."

"It is well you remind me what old friends we are," said Horace, very stern and cold.

"Yes; we shall neither of us ever forget that, I trust," Steven Pratman answered, looking fearlessly into the haggard, passionate face. "And one more question I want to ask. Is it a manly action of yours to leave your wife?"

"By Heaven!" cried Rohan, shaking his friend's hand from him as he might have shaken a poisonous touch, "you dare what no man shall dare twice to me! I have no wife. Whom do you mean by my wife? If any woman tells you she is a wife of mine, she lies—she lies as only a woman can!"

"I saw your marriage."

The words sounded calm and commonplace, as the lawyer framed them, in this new experiment of his; yet even he himself scarcely knew how hard it had been to utter them, while Horace, with that strange fierce light in his hollow eyes, yet seemed to look far off, and see nothing near him.

"There can be no hope," was the thought that fell heavily on Steven Pratman's heart, while Horace stood so poor, so proud, so wronged, in this joyless room; refusing all aid, spending his last night in his own country in the very keenest (because the most reticent) bitterness of solitude. "There would be more hope if he had loved her less wholly, less faithfully, even less honourably."

"You saw *what?*" queried Rohan, his lips scarce opening over the words, which ended with a laugh. "Don't you lie too, Steven. That is a woman's accomplishment—leave it to them. They do it so well—ah, so skilfully! We are no match for them there. What did you say? You saw what marriage? There was no marriage," he went on, the dazed look deepening in his eyes. "She went through the service—a holy service they had called it, too—using the name of a dead friend. Great God! Steven, when I recall that day, such a fire burns within my brain as—— But," with a sudden weary dropping of his passionate tone, "you could not understand."

And then Mr. Pratman was silent a little, for he *knew* he could not understand. But when he could trust himself to speak without a tremor in his voice, he asked another question.

"Rohan, where is Miss Carmichael?"

"Where is she?" echoed Horace, with a brief, sharp laugh. "At Hilton Guise, of course. Where else should Miss Carmichael be?"

"She has not gone to Hilton Guise yet," said Mr. Pratman, with slow emphasis; "and I think she never will go. I am thankful to know she has her own little income, for I do not believe she will ever touch a penny of the Hilton Guise property."

" Too *honourable!*" sneered Horace.

"Then," pursued the lawyer, gravely, " can you make no guess where she is ?"

"Oh! I could guess, if you wish it. She may be at Nice, concocting another little feminine deception.   She may be preparing herself to carry it out adroitly, and break another fool's heart."

A hot and angry retort rose to the lawyer's lips, but there it melted. How could he rebuke even the *suspicion* of a man whose suffering was so far beyond even his comprehension ?

"Horace," he said, very gravely—and Horace never guessed that the sympathy in his voice was for him, and not for the girl whose cause he pleaded with such per-sistency—"Horace, I cannot hear these things said of Evelyn Carmichael; nor would even you if you had heard her pitiful—ah, so sadly pitiful !—story of that night of their arrival in Nice, when Joyce Heringham died, and she was left so utterly alone—

not only in Nice, but in the world. The thought came very suddenly. It was in the sunset, she said, and somehow the sin looked not so dark or heavy then. She was wishing that it had been God's will that *she* had been the one to die, because Joyce could never have felt so utterly forsaken; and *her* death would have benefited one whom nothing in her life could ever benefit. Never by any deed *except her death* could she have benefited you. This thought flashed upon her, she said, and in one moment more——"

"I see," broke in Horace, with cold and cutting irony. "I know her, so of course I know how easy it must all have been. And afterwards, day by day, and week by week, it grew easier, as I grew to love her. Fool that I was, *how* I loved her! Every trifling word of hers was held so precious by me, and folded so tenderly in my heart, that now they burn into my memory, and—and, day and night, torture me to madness. I—I cannot for-

T 2

get. Forget!" he cried, with his hand tight upon his brow. "When will that be possible for me?"

"When you forgive," said Steven Pratman gently.

"Ah, yes, ah, yes!" cried Rohan, with a dry and sudden laugh. "And I shall forgive when I forget. Come, this is my last night, Steven. It was a pity I let you join me for so short a time. I have avoided you very dexterously, haven't I? Now and then some one told me—or was it only a thought of my own?—that you would not know me, even if you met me face to face in broad daylight, because I scarcely know my own face when I see it now. Age batters a man, I know; but, there's something *else* that strides through a century while age crawls through a year; and that leaves one in the darkness of the grave without the—the blessing of death. What—what is it, Steven? Why do you look at me so? Go out of this vile room. It is making a coward of *you*, and you are

not used to it as I am. You will not?
Then let us go together. It is a blusterous
night, but anything is better than staying
here and talking of—old times."

CHAPTER X.

FOR two years, Horace Rohan lived his busy and solitary life out in the New World. Then, from the slow torture of those years; from the long stern self-repression; from the unbroken tension of that defiant grip upon the heart of memory; there came slowly into birth a longing—vague and dim and shadowy, and yet so strong withal in every tiny fibre that, once sprung there, it held its place with sturdy resoluteness; until at last its tendrils clung resistlessly about his heart, and swayed him at their will.

Until at last, one day, from this indistinct, uncomprehended longing, there leaped into vivid, vigorous life one of those resolutions which, though they face us in-

stantaneously, take such a fixed and steadfast hold.

He knew well then what had been the
longing which for these two years he had
spurned and defied; and, when he owned this
to himself at last, he cried from his softened,
beating heart that he must see Evelyn once
again before it was too late; and, in forgiv-
ing, win forgiveness.

Poor as he was, he could still afford to
travel to the Old World and back, and win
a few words of pardon from her, with a
farewell hand-shake. Then he would leave
her in her beautiful home, with none of the
sad misgivings about his own future which he
—at last acknowledging to himself unconsciously how well he knew her—felt must
pain *her* now. And then he would come
back; and his work would be the lighter,
and his life a little less hard and cold and
useless, perhaps, for those last words she
would say to him.

* * * * * *

It was on one of those sweet and fair

Spring mornings when the air is laden with a subtle, dainty gladness, and every pulse within us throbs to a new life, rich with vague uncomprehended thankfulness, that Horace Rohan, weary of his city life afar; weary of his years of isolation and unrest; weary of the new fears and doubts which had haunted him during his voyage—as fears, unimagined before, *will* start and haunt us when we have once resolved upon our path—entered the wide fair domain surrounding his old home.

The woman who opened the park gates to him had received many a kindly word and glance from him in the old easy times, yet he passed her now unrecognised, an aged, worn, silent man. But a few minutes afterwards, in the great stillness and loveliness of the park, every spot of which he once had loved so dearly—in the fair tranquil beauty of the May morning—his eyes lost their stern, inlooking gaze, and knew at last—in that one moment of supreme emotion—the rare relief of tears.

* * * * * *

" Rohan, home again? Thank Heaven for that!"

There was a long, close hand-shake between the two old friends; and then Mr. Pratman walked on with Horace towards the old house, and chatted by the way, with no appearance of the effort that it cost him to hide his great surprise.

" I'm very tired of seeing the old home empty, Rohan."

" Empty?" echoed Horace, with a start.

"I daresay," remarked the lawyer placidly, " that it looks to you exactly as you left it, but no one has occupied it since that day. I come over myself, to keep everything straight and orderly, but no one else comes. I'm delighted that this chanced to be my morning for riding over. I had just put up my horse, and was going to have a talk with the steward—old Jennings still, Rohan, for not one of the old servants has been dismissed. They are all here still, as you can see by the bright, inhabited look of the house. And they are waiting for their master."

"But Miss Carmichael is here?" queried Horace, gazing intently at the window of one certain room which, two long years before, he had made so beautiful for his young wife.

"No, she has never been here. She calls this your property, and the only authority she exercises is the ordering it to be kept prepared for your return. The whole thing is a failure," the man of law added, with a sudden change of tone, as they walked on; "yet, fortunately, we have a kind of substitute for our non-resident squiress, and so, practically, we do not miss her. I will tell you all about it, only on that subject I don't think I could stand your contempt."

"What is it?" asked Horace wearily.

"Well, it is a most curious assertion to make, I know, Rohan, and you will naturally disbelieve it; but it is simple fact all the same. We have a little schoolmistress

at the Hilton School who cares for, and
knows and helps, not only the villagers,
but also the people on the Hilton Guise
estate. I see that you want to ask, with
your usual scepticism, what a young, and
not over-strong, village schoolmistress can
do to compensate for the absence of a
ruling power at the Hall; but I tell you
she does it. Simply by force of industry
and care and denial, backed by the rare
womanly advantages of tact and sympathy,
and that sweet charity which seeketh not
its own. There, that is enough of her," he
added, rather hurriedly, as he glanced into
Rohan's face, and missed the old disdain.
" I have to go through the village. Come
with me, and afterwards I will leave you
in peace here to wander alone till I am
ready. Come, and, if you are not bored, I
will show you what changes our schoolmistress has made. Nothing in the world
convinces like ocular demonstration. I might
talk to you for hours about our clubs and
institutes and societies; about our amuse-

ments (as well as instruction and benefits) for the poor; about our happy children and neat cottages; but you would not understand, as you would by a single visit. Don't interrupt me, Rohan. I'm not going to force this upon you. In old times you used to take an interest in the people, and I fancied you would still like to hear of their welfare."

"But it ought to be insured by the owner of Hilton Guise."

"Oh, never mind!" interpolated Mr. Pratman, coolly. "I daresay you won't object (when you see our schoolmistress) to her rather unusual conduct. It seems to fit her so very naturally that no one could object. She is ladylike, too, which partly accounts for her influence; and she has a small income of her own besides her salary, which partly accounts for her generosity. Horace," his old friend added, with a grave and even earnest change of tone, "one of the great hopes of my life will be fulfilled when you see for yourself what this girl's life has been, and hear the blessings that follow her on her quiet, solitary way."

"Why?" asked Horace, unconsciously moved by his friend's earnestness.

"Because it would be impossible for you, *after that*, to keep your old unfaith in woman. Do you see this new building? It is our school, Rohan, and, if you don't object, I will detain you here one minute. I want this paper given to the teacher. Here come the children trooping out. Aren't they a happy-looking, as well as an orderly, little regiment? And do you notice their pretty, fresh-looking uniform? This is all their teacher's doing, for the Rabys—kind as they are—were very content to let things be. Raby has a large family, you know, Rohan, and not the very richest living in the world."

"That will do," put in Horace, in a quick, troubled way. "Every word has a sting in it. And yet what can *I* do?"

Utterly heedless of Rohan's interruption,

Mr. Pratman stood with him in the play-ground, while the children, each with a bow or curtsey and a smile, trooped out of school. And, when he had let the younger ones all pass, he asked a quiet pleasant question of the elder ones who followed.

"I often see your teacher come out and play with you at this time. Where is she to-day?"

"Her head aches, sir," one of the girls answered, with frankness as well as respect. "She says it's nothing, only she liked to be left quiet for a bit."

"Rohan," said the lawyer, as the children passed on, "would you mind just going into the school-house for me with this paper, because I want to speak to Jenning's boy? It will save me a walk round by his father's cottage. Just give these papers to the schoolmistress; that is all. Here they are, and thank you for saving me these few minutes."

The long schoolroom, clean and neat
and fragrant with hawthorn, seemed to be
empty when Horace entered it; but still he
advanced and looked around him, with
that dreaminess in his steadfast grey eyes,
which had grown there through the solitude and sorrow of the last two years.
And there, at the far end of the room, he
saw a girl sitting, with her arms folded on
one of the desks, and her face hidden upon
them. It was a small, slight girlish figure,
yet Horace never for a moment fancied
this was one of the school-girls; the head
lay in a real childish abandonment of grief,
yet even in that first glance he knew it
was a woman who was suffering there.
Then suddenly his heart began to beat
with a passionate, resistless pain; and his
lips parted as if the drawn and quickened
breath were stifling him.

"*Evelyn !*"

The name, though only a whisper,
seemed in its low intensity to fill the silent

room, and Evelyn Carmichael lifted her
head, with a dazed, questioning glance,
while her hands were pressed upon her
temples. Then she saw *who* had called
her, and she stood mute a moment; her
bosom heaving passionately, and her slight
form tottering as she stood, her small
white face so full of weariness, and yet her
beautiful eyes still brave and patient.

"Evelyn! Oh, my love, forgive me!"

All the manliness of undying love, and
of heartfelt penitence, spoke in that involuntary cry. In all his heart there nestled
now no thought of blame for *her*. *His* was
the wrong—his only—and his only prayer
was for forgiveness.

"Horace," she said, her voice low and
broken, while her eyes read so wistfully
the face she loved, "have you forgiven
me? If so, this day will be—the best—
my life has ever known!"

"Oh, my love, it has been such a lonely
and unhappy life!" he cried, his eyes
growing dim with unaccustomed tears, as

he looked from the delicate, weary face round the long bare room. "Why are you here? Why do you give your life to others—*so*, when you could live in ease and luxury in your own home?"

"I have no other home," she answered, pressing both hands upon her beating heart. "I have no other home—unless you give me one. I shall never go from here—unless you forgive me, and—and take me to *your* home, as you—once—promised. Oh, Horace, I have loved you so —and suffered! Is—is it time we—should forgive—each other? And—after all— these years of——"

The words were never finished, for— folded close within her husband's arms at last—what words were needed?

*　　*　　*　　*　　*　　*

"It's quite absurd," remarked Mr. Pratman, " to suppose that we can do without our schoolmistress, now that we have all grown so ridiculously dependent upon her.

Besides, what claim have *you* upon her, Rohan? You told me you never married her."

"Raby will marry us to-morrow morning," said Horace. The lawyer had been shaking hands with Evelyn, his face full of delight; but Rohan took her back into his own possession at once; adding, with deep but subdued happiness within his eyes—" You will see that it is done properly this time, Steven, though no one else need be present. Then we will go somewhere, for my wife to get a little sunburnt; and then——"

"Home," put in Evelyn, softly, when he paused. "Oh, Horace, I wish it were not hard to you to speak of Hilton Guise as home!"

"Hard *now?*" he echoed, startling even himself by the new ring of gladness in his voice. "It will be the dearest spot on earth to me. But you have given me, this morning, the most precious gift in all the

world, dear wife, and I can think of nothing else just yet."

"But I can," observed Mr. Pratman,
composedly. "I can think how very
advisable it would be to give the school-
children a holiday."

END OF THE FIRST VOLUME.

LONDON: PRINTED BY DUNCAN MACDONALD, BLENHEIM HOUSE.

www.ingramcontent.com/pod-product-compliance
Lightning Source LLC
Chambersburg PA
CBHW031344070726
47496CB00017B/1651